The Merry-Go-Round

The
Merry-Go-Round

Donna Fasano

Find the author:

Facebook – Facebook.com/DonnaFasanoAuthor

Twitter – Twitter.com/DonnaFaz

Pinterest – Pinterest.com/DonnaFaz

Instagram – Instagram.com/Donna_Fasano

Newsletter Sign-up – http://madmimi.com/signups/110899/join

First Edition: December 2009

Second Edition: October 2011

Third Edition: October 2017

Contents

When Lauren divorces her husband, she has one thought on her mind... stepping off the merry-go-round. However, her life quickly turns into a three-ring circus: her hypochondriac father moves in, her ex is using her shower when she's not home, and her perky assistant is pushing her out into the fearsome dating world. She also has to decide if the dilapidated barn and vintage merry-go-round she is awarded in the divorce settlement is a blessing or a bane. As if Lauren's personal life isn't chaotic enough, this slightly jaded attorney is overrun with a cast of quirky characters who can't stay on the right side of the law. What's a woman to do? She can allow life to spin her in circles forever. Or she can reach out and grab the brass ring.

Chapter One

You don't know a woman
till you've met her in court.
~ Norman Mailer

"It's a great day for a divorce." Lauren took a quick look around to see if anyone had heard her talking to herself before she hurried up the courthouse steps. If everything went according to plan, she would walk out of this building a free woman. She'd sleep a lot better and breathe a lot easier minus the hundred and eighty pounds of man meat she'd been lugging around for far too long.

A blessed blast of cool air billowed from the building when she hauled open the plate glass door. Although it was a few days into September, the hot, humid temperatures that had plagued Sterling through the lazy months of summer were stubbornly hanging on. She lifted her hand in greeting to Rusty as he tucked the floor polisher into the janitorial closet; she nodded to colleagues she met in the hallway. The reverberation of her high heels clicking against the marble floor had her smiling. It was a satisfying sound—one she'd heard nearly every workday since she'd passed the Maryland Bar and ordered the door plaque that read Lauren E. Hunkavic, Attorney At Law.

Of course, it was Flynn now. The name change was about the only good thing that had come from her marriage. Not that she wasn't proud of her maiden name. Her Czechoslovakian great-grandparents had risked everything, left everyone they loved in search of a new life across the ocean. But kids were mean. And mercilessly unrelenting. Every Halloween she had been saddled with Hunk-a-trick. The summer she went through a chubby stage, it had been Hunk-a-thick. She lost the weight and they'd come up with Hunk-a-stick. She hadn't gone on a single Saturday movie outing with friends that she hadn't heard Hunk-a-flick at least once. Missing a couple of days of school turned her into Hunk-a-sick. Although the teasing during her adolescence had been mostly innocuous, it had been endless and irritating as hell. Her parents and teachers alike had explained that the kids were simply goading her into reacting. "They're paying for a ticket," her dad had told her, "but you don't have to put on a show." High school seemed to mature most of her peers, but there had been a moron or two who just seemed to get crueler and nastier in their twisting of her last name.

Turning the corner, she wasn't surprised to see her father sitting on the bench near the elevator. His beat up Dodge Ram had been parked on West Main Street directly in front of the courthouse steps. He must have arrived at daybreak to bag the prime spot. Even though she was ten minutes early for their court appointment—the first slot of the day—Lauren had been forced to use the side lot.

She tried to gauge her father's mood as she got closer. If Eeyore ever took sick in the 100 Acre Wood, Lew Hunkavic would be the perfect stand-in for the pessimistic Equus asinus.

"Hey there, Dad. You look good this morning. All bright-eyed and bushy-tailed. You must have slept well."

Asking her dad how he was feeling held too great a possibility of opening a huge can of big, fat blood worms. Instead, she made a habit of making the most positive assessment possible.

"My hair hurts." He raked his stubby fingers through the thatch of silver covering his scalp, tilting his head and wincing as he did so. "Been hurting for days. You'da known about it if you'da called."

"Dad, we had dinner on Sunday," she reminded him lightly. "It's only Wednesday."

"I know what day of the week it is," he groused.

She punched the elevator call button. "Come the weekend, you won't have to worry about me calling you, will you?" A slight movement had her eyes darting to his face. She'd thought she'd seen his mouth quirk, but surely she was mistaken. He had to be as dismayed about these circumstances as she.

"Besides that," she continued, "your hair can't hurt."

He rose from the bench, the rubber tip of his cane squeaking on the polished stone floor.

"Hair is made up of nothing but dead cells, Dad. No nerve endings, no pain."

He glowered, his gray-green eyes narrowing on

her, just as the elevator dinged, the up arrow lit and the doors slid open. "It's carbunculosis."

They stepped inside and Lauren touched the button that would take them to the third floor.

"An infection of the scalp. I researched it at that website I told you about. All Natural Health dot org."

The internet. It was both a blessing and a bane. A person could find information about anything there. Anything.

Most people spent their golden years traveling the country, or engrossed in some well-loved hobby, or immersed in great works of literature. Not her seventy-year-old dad. Oh, no. He spent his days hunched over a keyboard, trolling the Web for medical maladies with which to label every ache and pain he experienced.

Softly, she warned, "Dad, it wouldn't hurt to get a professional opinion."

He straightened. "You telling me my scalp isn't sore?"

"I'm not saying that at all." Suddenly, Lauren realized she'd better back-pedal a bit. She needed her dad in good spirits this morning. Well, as good as his spirits could be, anyway.

The doors slid open and they exited the elevator.

"I have no doubt you're hurting," she told him. "I can see by the look on your face. Maybe you should go see Dr. Amos."

"Charlie Amos is a dimwit."

"Dad, you and Dr. Amos have been friends for—"

"I don't need a doctor, Lauren. I bought myself some tea tree oil. A few drops in my shampoo should take care of the problem."

"Tea tree oil, huh?" She stifled the sigh building at the base of her diaphragm. "Where'd you hear about that? Find A Cure dot com?" Before he could respond, she said, "Dad, you need to forgive Doc."

"Bless my butt and call me Betty. The man couldn't diagnose a simple rash, Lauren." Lew shook his head in disgust. "Dry skin, my ass. I knew I had a problem, and I found a cure, too. That old quack can't even turn on a computer, let alone do a Google search. He's way behind the times. How can he ever expect to keep up with advances in health care?"

Medical journals, maybe? Professional conferences? Refresher courses? But Lauren zipped her lip.

The fact was that the good doctor had had the

gall to warn her father not to take everything he read on the Net as gospel truth. That had been four months ago, and since then her dad had refused to acknowledge Dr. Amos existed.

They arrived at the double doors of the courtroom, and Lauren spun to face her father.

"Okay, Dad—" she lifted her free hand, palm up "—can we set this aside for now? This is very important to me."

The deep sigh he emitted could have been his reluctance to veer off the topic of his latest infirmity, or it could have been his reaction to the court petition she'd filed. Either way, she felt it best to ignore his gloom.

"We've gone over what the judge might ask you, right?" She dipped her chin, arched her brows, straightening the collar of his royal blue dress shirt. "You remember how to respond, yes?"

"Lauren, I'm not a four year old."

She gave him a small smile, smoothing the fabric of his shirt. "Sorry, Dad."

Her attaché thumped against the door of courtroom number three as she grabbed the handle. The room was empty and quiet as they made their way up the center aisle and took seats at the plaintiff's table. Lauren snapped open her soft leather case and pulled out the file containing her divorce papers.

Papers that were missing a vital signature. And it wasn't hers.

She spent a few minutes studying her notes and mulling over all the arguments and rebuttals that might arise. The court clerk entered from one of the two doors located behind the judge's bench, perused the room and then ducked back inside the office.

"The judge must be ready to start," Lauren told her father, glancing at her watch. One minute before nine. "It's just like Greg to be late. Never takes a single thing seriously." Dipping her gaze to her notes again, she murmured, "He's probably rescuing some poor, decrepit soul out there somewhere." If there were a poor, decrepit soul within a hundred mile radius of Sterling, Greg would find it, that was certain.

A few minutes later, the door at the main entrance to the courtroom swung open and Greg waltzed in. Lauren forced herself not to turn around, keeping her eyes glued to the documents in front of her. But she could see his loose, breezy stride in her mind's eye. And she could easily imagine his attire: battered, steel-toed Wolverines, worn blue jeans and t-shirt. If he'd decided to dress up for the occasion, he might have gone all out and donned a polo shirt.

With her arm firmly twisted behind her back, she'd have admitted the fact that, when they'd first met Greg's blue-collar style had appealed to her. He was different from the men she'd dated—the studious collegians that had made up her social circle while she'd earned her law degree.

Soft, worn denim had the ability to hug a man's rear like no other fabric. And the physical nature of Greg's work tightened his glutes to pinch-tempting firmness. The memory had heat flushing Lauren's face.

She'd grown adept at ignoring her husband altogether. The practice had kept her sane for months now. But to force those inappropriate images from her brain, she lifted her gaze to the empty court clerk's desk and snipped, "It's good that some people finally decided to show up."

"Good morning to you, too, Lauren."

He stood next to her, close enough that the familiar scent of him—bath soap and sunshine—forced the muscles of her belly to tense involuntarily. She felt him move away, heard him take a seat at the defendant's table, and that's when she stole a glance. His skin was tanned to a deep golden olive, his black-as-night hair slicked back from his morning shower, his even blacker eyes staring directly at her. She redirected her gaze as casually as possible.

"How you doing, Lew?" Greg asked her father.

"Got carbunculosis. My hair is damn sore."

"That's a shame."

Lauren couldn't quite keep from rolling her eyes at the sympathy in Greg's tone. Like he really cared. But then she sobered because she knew he truly did. About her dad, at least. Ever since she'd introduced the two men, they'd been fast friends. Of all the gripes she had against Greg, his treatment of her father would never be one of them.

"You running a fever?" Greg scooted his chair a bit as he spoke.

"Nah." Lew shook his head. "Nothing like that. I'm sure adding a little anti-bacterial oil to my shampoo will fix me right up."

As appreciative as she'd always been of Greg's concern for and patience with her dad, she was just too annoyed with the man right now to show it. She picked up her file folder and legal pad and tapped them smartly on the table. "I see you came prepared, as usual."

No documents. No notepad. Not even a carpenter's pencil tucked behind his ear. Looks as though he'd given today's court appearance as much attention as the divorce petition she'd served him with.

She sensed rather than saw his mouth draw into a slow smile.

Softly, he replied, "Hey, I'm here, aren't I?"

Before she could offer a biting retort, the court clerk appeared.

"All rise," the woman said, just as Judge Brooks opened the door of his office. "Court is now in session. The Honorable Matthew Brooks presiding."

A tall man in his sixties, Judge Brooks had salt and pepper hair and ruddy cheeks. He was one of three judges in Sterling, which meant he presided over a third of the legal proceedings that filtered through the courthouse and that he and Lauren saw each other often. She knew him to be smart and open-minded and fair. He slipped into his black leather chair, set down the papers he was carrying and smiled at each of them in turn.

"Mrs. Flynn, I've read your complaint," the judge

said, "and from what I can see here, you don't really have a legal leg to stand on. But I agreed to meet with all parties concerned today because I'm sure you intend to try to change my mind."

Ready for a fight, Lauren stood. "Judge, if you'll allow me to explain. It's been a full year since I—"

Judge Brooks lifted a hand. "Hold on, Counselor. I'm not finished."

She sat down, murmuring a quick, "Pardon me."

The man propped his elbows on the desk, fisted his hands and focused on Lauren. "Your frustration is made quite clear in your complaint. But you know the law, Mrs. Flynn." He stared at the documents in front of him then looked up at her again. "Do you mind if I ask you a few questions?"

She knew Matthew Brooks' 'fatherly lecture' tone when she heard it. But she was willing to suffer through a mild scolding for wasting the court's time if it meant she'd have a chance to argue her grievance in the end. And he was too fair not to hear her out.

"I don't mind at all, Judge," she said.

The clerk stood, but the judge shook his head. "There'll be no swearing in today. We're just chatting this morning. This meeting has about as much legal binding as if we were sitting across the street at Rose's Diner." He looked at Lauren and asked, "I read that you and Gregory Flynn have been living separately and apart without cohabitation for twelve months. But what I want to know is this; did your husband commit adultery?"

"No, Your Honor," she said.

"Did he desert you?"

"No. I was the one who asked him to leave."

"Was he convicted of a crime?"

Does costing me every last nickel of savings count as a crime? she wanted to rail. Does breaking my heart count? Does making me cry until I puked count? How about disillusioning me? Or pissing me off beyond all reason? None of those charges being convictable offenses, all she curtly replied was, "No, he wasn't."

"Is Gregory Flynn insane?"

She went still and then glanced over at the man in question, seeing his dark eyes glitter, and then he gave her one of those devil-may-care smiles of his. Her heart fluttered at the same instant that her ire flared. Damn, but the man irritated her. She couldn't believe that not so long ago she'd found that grin highly arousing. Automatically, her litigation training kicked in and she refrained from glaring at him. Turning to Judge Brooks once again, she hesitated a few long seconds before answering, "No. Not in any certifiable way, that is."

Ignoring her quip, the judge queried, "Has he abused you?"

That all depended on a person's definition of abuse. He'd abused her bank account; he'd battered her heart; he'd pummeled to death her idea of a good and solid man-woman relationship. Lauren thought she just might be able to argue this point and win, but keeping her focus on the goal of completely severing all ties to Greg here, now, today, she forced herself to answer, "He hasn't."

"And we wouldn't be here at all," the judge said quietly, "if this separation were voluntary. Isn't that true, Mrs. Flynn?"

"It is."

The day she had told Greg he had to pack his things and leave she'd never been angrier in her life. He'd argued with her that they could work things out, but she'd stood firm. If she'd been raised just a tad differently, she'd have surrendered to her fury that day; she'd have screamed bloody murder and tossed his clothes out on the front lawn; she'd have—

Now was not the time to get lost in pleasant daydreams.

"According to Maryland law, if the separation were voluntary, the divorce would be final after twelve months." Judge Brooks lowered his clasped hands and leaned forward. "As I said before, Mrs. Flynn, I understand that you're frustrated. You've been waiting a year for your husband to agree to a divorce. That's a long time. It's logical, even reasonable, that you'd want to get on with your life. However, I must remind you that since this is an involuntary separation, and that Mr. Flynn has every legal right to wait the full two years allowed by law before signing those papers."

Lauren popped up from her seat. "But there's no need to wait, your Honor. There is absolutely, positively no possibility of reconciliation. None. Nada." She swiped her flattened palm through the air. "Zip."

Flipping open her file, she glanced at her notes. Going over things in an orderly manner was crucial. "I brought my father as a fact witness. He'll be happy to testify that Greg and I aren't getting back together."

"Mrs. Flynn, sit down," the Judge said quietly.

"Relax. Whether or not you'll be getting back together doesn't matter. The law states—"

"I know what the law states." Judge Brooks cast her a narrowed-eyed warning and she clamped her lips shut. She lowered herself onto her seat as he'd ordered, muttering, "I'm sorry I interrupted you. It won't happen again."

The judge studied her a moment and then turned his resigned gaze to her father. "Mr. Hunkavic?"

"Yes, sir." Her dad sat up straighter, his fingers curled on the knob of his cane. "That's me. Lewis Ivan Hunkavic."

"Do you feel, Mr. Hunkavic, that your daughter and son-in-law have any chance of working out their differences?"

"Well, your Honor, sir."

The odd hitch in her dad's tone had Lauren turning toward him. He combed his fingers through his hair, his bushy brows pulling together.

"My first concern is Lauren's happiness, of course," Lew began. He paused, then added, "I know what she wants me to say to you. She's yammered at me about it numerous times."

Her lips parted and she sucked in a silent gasp.

"You're not sworn in, Mr. Hunkavic," Judge

Brooks explained, "but that doesn't mean I wouldn't appreciate complete honesty here."

She watched her dad hesitate a moment, then he did the most peculiar thing. He reached down with his free hand, grasped the arm of his chair and scooted it the merest fraction of an inch—away from her.

"Sir, I have to admit," he said, his gaze trained on the judge, "my daughter tends to be a tad stubborn. She inherited that trait from her mother."

The judge smiled just as Lew quietly added, "God rest her soul."

"Excuse me for butting in, Judge." Lauren stood again, her voice loud and clear. "But I think my father's about to become a hostile witness."

"Mrs. Flynn, you promised you wouldn't interrupt. And might I remind you that you requested this meeting? This is an informal gathering." As if confirming the remark, Judge Brooks reached over and slid the gavel a few inches to his right. "We're just chatting here. That's all we're doing."

Lauren sat again, casting her father a withering look even though she knew it would have no effect on the old coot whatsoever. There were times when Lew Hunkavic could be as infuriating as her husband, and she could feel in her bones that this was surely going to be one of them.

"You were saying, Mr. Hunkavic?" Judge Brooks said.

Lew tapped his cane silently against the floor twice. "Sir, I believe my daughter is very angry with Greg. With good reason, I'll give her that. He's made a few mistakes over the past couple of years." He leaned forward, softening his voice even further. "But, personally, I don't think money is a good reason to end a marriage."

Again, Lauren sucked in a sharp breath. "Dad! There's more to this than money. You know that."

She faced forward, ignoring the men on either side of her. "Your Honor, there is no possibility of reconciliation for Gregory Flynn and myself. I can guarantee this. It takes two to tango, and not only am I unwilling to dance, I can no longer hear the music." Stiffly, she added, "The fact that I had to sell my tap shoes to pay my husband's debt is only one reason our marriage fell apart."

Beside her, Lew murmured, "Did you ever think that was part of the problem between you and Greg? You insisted on tangoing in tap shoes?"

Lauren took no notice of her father's questions, focusing only on making her point. "Judge Brooks,

I emptied my savings and pension funds in order to pay Greg's debts. He's cost me nearly sixty thousand dollars. My father will be moving in with me at the end of the week because I can no longer afford to pay his rent and save for my retirement at the same time."

"Thanks for telling the world I'm a kept man," her dad said.

"I'm not keeping you, Dad. I'm helping you. There's a big difference." She glanced over at Greg and saw him staring straight ahead, the muscle near his temple so tense it looked painful. His embarrassment didn't concern her. She wanted his signature on those papers, damn it.

"Judge," she continued, "it will take me years to recoup my losses. Every time I sit down to pay bills and realize that I have to trim my budget even further due to Greg's poor financial planning, his stupid business choices, I get sick to my stomach. My nausea only increases when I remember how he lied. He betrayed my trust. I want this over with. Once and for all and forever." She snapped her jaw shut and offered Judge Brooks a look of unwavering determination.

The elderly man in the formidable black robe returned her gaze, and she worried that he might disappoint her. But then he shook his head ever so slightly and turned to Greg.

And that's when Lauren could almost taste victory.

"Mr. Flynn," Judge Brooks said softly, "do you mind if I ask you why you're dragging your heels on this thing?"

Lauren watched Greg ponder the question for a moment.

Finally, he lifted his burly shoulders a fraction, raised one calloused hand, palm up, and said, "Pride, I guess."

The judge tapped his fingertips soundlessly on his desktop. "Your answer surprises me. I was expecting to hear something altogether different. Can you help me understand what you mean?"

A tall, solid man used to handling a miter saw or climbing around on roofing trusses, Greg looked uncomfortable in the hard-angled, wooden chair. However, it could have been the question he found discomfiting.

"I don't like the idea of leaving things like this."

When he hesitated, the judge coaxed, "What do you mean, Mr. Flynn? Leave things like what?"

Greg cleared his throat and shifted his weight in the chair. "I, uh, I don't like the idea of walking away from Lauren while things are... well, such a mess. If she'd accept my calls, or talk to me when she sees me on the street, I could have saved us from having to come here today. I could have expressed my feelings to her. Explained my plan. I was hoping to work things out." He splayed his hands on the tabletop. "Not that I think we'll get back together or anything like that, Judge. Lauren's made that clear enough." He pondered a moment, scrubbing at his jaw. "But I wanted to work out the business end of things. It would be humiliating for me to agree to divorce my wife while I still owe her so much money. You're a man, I'm sure you can understand that."

Lauren blinked. "But you don't owe me any money." Confusion weakened her tone. She looked at the judge and firmly stated, "He doesn't owe me any money."

"That's what I tried to tell him," Lew said under his breath.

"Oh, but I do." The resolve in Greg's words was as strong as hers and it drew her attention. He faced her, had turned his entire body to address her as if she were the only person in the room. "You said it yourself, Lauren. Nearly sixty thousand dollars."

"But, Greg, my name was on the business." Boy, had that been a mistake. But love had a way of making a person as blind as a mole rat. "That was my share of the debt when the store went under."

"That was my debt, Lauren. Not yours."

The intensity of his onyx eyes threatened to suck her in, swallow her whole. This was exactly why she'd turned and walked in the opposite direction whenever she'd spied him in the Super G or at the County Bank. She couldn't talk to the man without feeling she might come apart at the seams.

"Your Honor—" She concentrated on the man in the black robe—the one person who had some semblance of a chance of tipping the balance and winning her freedom. "Will you please explain the law to him? Make him see that he does not owe me any money?"

Judge Brooks' expression had lightened significantly as Greg had talked. "You have to admit, Mrs. Flynn, that your husband's motives are genuine. He's looking out for your best interest." He shrugged. "I'd even go so far as to say Mr. Flynn is being downright chivalrous in the matter."

Lauren frowned. "No disrespect intended, but chivalry died along with King Arthur."

"There you go again," Lew grumbled, "tangoing in tap shoes."

Glancing over her shoulder, she said, "That makes absolutely no sense. Can you sit there quietly? If you refuse to help my case, Dad, the least you can do is not hurt it." He looked wounded, but her determination was building and she didn't want to lose the momentum. She swung her gaze to the judge. "I don't want Mr. Flynn's money. I want his signature. On these documents." She waved the papers in the air. "I don't want to wait another year for my divorce. I need to—"

"All right, already!" Greg smacked the tabletop and stood, the legs of his chair grating against the floor. "If it's that important to you, Lauren, I'll sign the papers."

Yes! This was what she'd been hoping for. That Greg would finally understand her vexation and agree to dissolve their marriage, once and for all.

She snatched up her Montblanc and set the petition in front of Greg with rocket speed. His rough fingertips grazed the back of her hand when he reached for the ink pen; heated electricity skittered across her skin forcing her to suppress a shiver. He showed no sign of noticing.

"You should read them before signing," she

murmured, overwhelmed with satisfaction as she watched him scrawl his name on the line.

He set down the pen, his severe gaze raking her face. "Thanks for the advice, Counselor."

Ignoring his disgruntled tone, Lauren picked up documents. "Judge Brooks, may I approach the bench? If you sign these now, it will expedite the process even further."

"Hold up a minute, Mrs. Flynn." The judge opened the manila file sitting on his desk. "This changes everything. We have property to take care of. We might as well do it now since we're all present."

She paused, her heart fluttering. "I beg your pardon, Judge, but there's nothing to divvy up. I bought the house before we married. Greg's name was never on the deed." Lauren couldn't count the number of times she'd thanked the heavens for that bit of saving grace. "All the inventory was liquidated and the store was sold, and it took everything to pay the business debts. I kept my car. He kept his truck. And I agreed he should keep his tools so he could earn a living." She straightened the documents in her hands, tapped them on the table. "So you can see, there's nothing else left to split."

The Merry-Go-Round

"Oh, Mrs. Flynn," the judge almost sang the words while he shuffled through the papers in front of him, "now there's where you're wrong."

Chapter Two

Life is tough, but it's tougher when you're stupid.
~ John Wayne

"**Y**ou will never guess what Greg did." Lauren slapped her attaché onto her desktop and continued without waiting for a reply from the woman who'd followed her into her office. "He hid a piece of property from me."

Norma Jean Pruitt's brown eyes went round. At sixty-two going on thirty, Norma Jean had been with Lauren since the first week that the office had been open for business. She'd hired on as Lauren's receptionist, and over the years, had added differentials to her job description until she'd included a myriad of professional and personal titles, the most important of which was close-friend-and-confidant. Norma Jean's vibrant energy hummed like a live wire; clients and colleagues alike often commented on the woman's joie de vivre when they came into the office. She could instill hope in the dispirited, dry the tears of the dejected, spark courage in the fearful... she was like some sort of superhero for the soul. The practice didn't bring in enough money to pay the woman the buckets of gold she was worth.

"It's over an acre of ground out on Skeeter Neck Road."

Norma Jean's nose wrinkled. "Not the best part of town."

Lauren pulled out her divorce file and handed it over. "Tell me about it."

Norma Jean accepted the folder, tucked it under the ever present legal pad she cradled. "I thought everything was sold off when the hardware store went bust. How could he still have a piece of property?"

"Apparently," Lauren said, tugging out several other folders and setting them on her desk, "he renovated someone's house and it turned out the person couldn't pay. Not in cash, anyway." Her tone grated as she asked, "Is anyone surprised?

Where does he find these people?" She sighed. "Anyway, Greg accepted the land as payment when it was offered. A barter, he told the judge."

"Skeeter Neck Road runs through a lot of low, swampy land." Norma moved to the window. "He's not building a house out there, is he?" She adjusted the blinds to block out most of the sun's glare.

"He sure isn't." Lauren set her attaché behind her desk. "Because Judge Brooks awarded the property to me."

Norma spun around to face her. "What? Really?"

She nodded. "Greg tried to argue that the plot of ground wasn't actual income; that he'd made the deal after we'd separated. That it shouldn't come into play in any settlement. And that it wasn't worth anything given its location and that the only thing on it was a dilapidated shed. But he'd already set himself up for a fall by telling the judge that he's been stalling on the divorce because he didn't want to end the marriage owing me so much money."

Forever the romantic, Norma Jean said, "Awww…" Her brown eyes softened, her ruby lips parting slightly. "You have to admit, Lauren, that's kind of sweet."

Lauren just shook her head. What was it with

people? They couldn't see the truth about Greg even when it was staring them right in the face.

"Judge Brooks awarded me the land, the shed and all its contents. Then he ordered his clerk to file my divorce papers within the next five business days. And he told Greg he was to deliver the deed to the land to me by then." She sat down in her desk chair and slid her knees under the desk. "So next week I'll be officially divorced and the owner of a plot of land out on Skeeter Neck Road." Absently, she reached for the folders in front of her and snatched up her pen, muttering, "Why do I have this feeling that I'll be free of one albatross only to find myself saddled with another?"

"Now, Lauren," Norma Jean scolded. "Don't be so pessimistic."

* * *

A rawboned young man, Scotty Shaw had big hands and knobby shoulders he had yet to grow into. His Ichabod Crane neck looked ill fitted to support his large head. Had he more meat on his long-boned body, Lauren would have taken him for a running back or a wide receiver; however, there didn't appear to be enough muscle and sinew to carry his six foot frame let alone make him a college football star.

He shifted gracelessly in the leather wing-backed chair, his bony knees veering together then sliding apart as Lauren glanced over the police report he'd brought with him. She read the facts, pursing her lips tightly to keep from smiling. Sometimes she struggled not to laugh at the antics that landed these kids into trouble.

What were you thinking? was the first question she wanted to ask. But she knew better. It was obvious that Scotty Shaw—and every other Sterling University student who showed up on her doorstep in dire need of legal representation due to a single moment of stupid, rash or reckless indiscretion—hadn't thought about the possible consequences of his actions.

"So, Scott," she began, "you were arrested and charged with Disorderly Conduct—"

"I was just walking down the street, minding my own business. I swear." His slate blue eyes went wide, giving him a little-boy-lost look.

"—and Alarm and Offense—"

"I never touched that lady or her husband with my..." He paused, two fire engine-red patches splotching his hollow cheeks. He scooted to sit straighter. "I swear I didn't. You have to believe me. She's the one who made contact. I was just standing there minding my own business, waiting for the light to change so I could cross the street." His gaze shifted nervously. "She's the one who started the conversation. She's the one who reached out and slid her hand up the—" He stopped again. Swallowed. "Up my—" Another pause. He frowned. "Her husband went absolutely ballistic when she touched it."

It in this case being a five foot plastic, blow up penis, 'complete with furry scrotum' the arresting officer had noted in his report, which Scotty had carted under his arm the full length of Main Street on his way to a Saturday night frat party. Had he remained on University property with his indecent paraphernalia, his only probable consequence would have been a reprimand from the Dean of Discipline. But several town residents had become involved in the ensuing altercation, not to mention the Sterling police who tended to be tough on the college kids, taking the stance that cracking down early in the fall semester meant fewer offenses later on in the year. The hardnosed attitude of town law enforcement toward the students provided Lauren with a hefty chunk of her yearly income.

"The guy shoved me away from his wife, whipped out his cell and dialed 911 before I could take a breath. I tried to run, but he grabbed my arm and wouldn't let go. He was strong for an old dude." One knee began to bounce. "And the car accident wasn't my fault, either. That woman should have been paying attention to traffic; not gawking at what was happening on the sidewalk."

Lauren sighed. A pedestrian incident and a traffic accident. Scott had caused a lot of paperwork for the Sterling PD. The attending officer must have been totally ticked to pile on the charges like this. Looking up from the arrest report, she asked, "And you resisted arrest because...?"

The young man's jaw jutted with affront. "I didn't mean to resist anything. That cop threatened to poke a hole in my... in the..." Frustration knitted Scott's brow and he went quiet. Finally, he exhaled, his shoulders sagging. When he spoke, his anger seemed to have fizzled.

"I just lost my head, is all. I wasn't thinking. I was furious that those cops could just take something that belonged to me. Something that cost me a whole week's allowance, Ms. Flynn. And that's not including postage and handling."

His chin dipped as he sulked. "It's all Brian's fault. He borrowed my bike pump last week and never brought it back. Then he wouldn't answer his cell on Saturday. I must have rang him two dozen times. I couldn't go to the party without seeing what it looked like first, you know? But Brian was off doing who knows what." He shook his head, shoving his hair off his forehead in frustration. "So I ended up blowing it up myself." Scotty's blue eyes met hers, pleading for understanding. "It took forever. I thought I'd pass out. I couldn't let the air out after working so freakin' hard to inflate it. So I decided to just take it to the party." He shrugged and gazed off toward the window as he murmured, "What harm could it do?"

She rested her elbow on the desk and pressed her curled index finger to her lips. Troubled clients often took her silence as sympathy, and that was okay with her at the moment as Scott was obviously feeling lower than low. However, conjuring compassion for someone who had pulled such an idiotic prank was difficult. Besides that, she was struggling not to chuckle. Had he honestly thought he could carry a five foot plastic penis down Main Street in broad daylight and not catch trouble from someone?

Her breath left her in another quiet sigh. At

times, youth and inexperience made perfectly intelligent people act like idiots. As Lauren pulled open a side drawer on her desk and took out a yellow legal pad, she said, "I'll need an eighteen hundred dollar retainer."

"Eighteen hundred dollars?"

She didn't take offense at his tone; she'd heard it hundreds of times before from people who sat in that very chair.

"Scott, I need a couple hours to research case law. Then I'll need an hour, maybe longer, to prepare my argument in case I have to offer one. And we'll be in court up to three hours waiting for your case to be heard."

"But I don't have that kind of money. I'm a full-time student. I don't have a job. My dad gives me fifty bucks a week spending allowance." His big hands tensed on the arms of the chair. "Do you think I could get away with going to court without a lawyer?"

"I wouldn't recommend it." She picked up her pen and clicked it three times. "All the charges are misdemeanors, but each one carries a maximum sentence that includes a fine plus jail time."

Scott's pale face went paler. "Jail? I could go to jail?"

She nodded. "It's not all that likely since it's a first offense, but you can never tell with these things. And you did resist arrest. That tends to make the judge less forgiving."

His breathing accelerated.

"Scott—" she set down her pen and laced her fingers on top of the legal pad "—have you called your parents?"

"It's just my dad." He paused the merest fraction of a second before softly adding, "For the most part." He looked at her, unblinkingly. "Anyway, I was hoping I could get through this on my own. Dad'll kill me if he finds out about this."

It's just my dad. For the most part. Lauren wondered what that meant exactly.

She tilted her head a fraction, smiling. "I seriously doubt your father would take things that far. He might be disappointed, and none of us wants to disappoint our parents. But sometimes that can't be helped, Scott. You need some support. Emotionally and financially." She flattened her mouth apologetically. "I can hold your hand. I can talk you through the legalities of your situation. But, unfortunately, I can't work for free. You won't find a lawyer in this town who will."

Sure, she'd like to be a do-gooder, a good Samaritan who cast aside all responsibility to help out every Tom, Dick and Scotty in need. Who wouldn't? But she had people depending on her. Norma Jean needed the paycheck Lauren wrote every week. There was office rent, a car lease and house mortgage to pay, not to mention utilities. And her father needed her help. She needed an income.

Lauren blinked a couple of times when she realized her blood had begun to simmer. Her jaw was clenched. She gulped in a deep, relaxing breath, realizing, too, that the anger roiling through her wasn't this young man's fault.

No, it sure wasn't. Her financial situation was no one's fault but Greg's.

She stood and smiled, offering her hand to Scott. "As Norma Jean explained, your initial consultation is free. Your court date is weeks away. You've got plenty of time to decide what you want to do."

He rose from the chair, shook her hand. "Thanks for your time," he murmured.

The fear and confusion shadowing his gaze spurred a gentleness in her. "This isn't the end of the world, Scott."

He nodded, but looked clearly unconvinced.

"Call your father. I'm sure he'd want to hear from you. I'll bet he'll be more understanding than you imagine. But whether you do or not, I can't urge you strongly enough to hire a lawyer. As I said, it doesn't have to be me. But going to court without legal representation wouldn't be wise."

He nodded again and then walked toward the door.

She said his name and he turned to face her. Lauren hoped her next statement didn't sound heartless, but she could no more have left it unsaid than she could have stopped breathing.

"If you do decide to hire me, you'll have to bring a check with you the next time you come."

Scotty Shaw left her office looking like a whipped puppy.

Chapter Three

Marriage is a three ring circus:
engagement ring, wedding ring and suffering.
~ Unknown

Skeeter Neck Road dipped and twisted its way through the western Maryland countryside. Black chokeberry, thorn bushes, and other weedy scrub carpeted the swampy areas, and what sounded like an army of frogs serenaded Lauren as she drove with her windows down. Where the land was elevated, she passed small stands of trees; pine, butternut, ash, and sumac.

Driving out to find a piece of property she didn't exactly own just yet was probably the last thing she should be doing this morning. She should have stayed home, enjoying a second cup of coffee while reading the Saturday edition of the paper. Like everyone else did these days, Lauren got most of her news from on-line sites, but there was something about newsprint that felt just right for laid-back Saturday mornings. The point was, she should be relaxing, reveling in her last hours of solitude before her dad moved in with her later today.

Lauren rubbed her fingertips back and forth across her forehead. She loved her dad dearly and would have done anything for him. But the two of them hadn't lived under the same roof in years. He'd lived alone since she'd moved out to attend college, and with the break up of her marriage, Lauren's home life had been pretty solitary for the past year as well. This new living arrangement wasn't going to be easy. For either of them.

Yes, she should be home enjoying the last vestiges of peace and quiet she would have in the foreseeable future. However, curiosity had spurred her out the door on this glorious morning. She'd contacted a friend in the deed registry office yesterday for the exact location of the property she'd been awarded by Judge Brooks.

She kept glancing at the dashboard, and when

the odometer hit eight point five miles, she slowed the car. According to her friend, the property was located on the east side of Skeeter Neck Road just under nine miles out of town.

Her father had called Thursday night, grousing at her about taking what he felt was Greg's property.

"Just because the judge gave it to you," he'd said, "doesn't mean you have to accept it."

Lauren had succeeded in keeping her tone sweet as she'd replied, "And leave you explaining to everyone in town that you raised an idiot? Dad, I'd never do that to you."

Braking the car to a crawl, she inched past a dirt drive and craned her neck to see around the trees fronting the patch of land. A large barn took center stage; she could make out bare wood showing through faded red paint in spots on the building. She drove on, looking for a plot with a shed as Greg had described to the judge this week.

She passed a field that stretched into next week, a recent harvesting having left behind row upon row of some kind of plant stubs. When the odometer hit ten miles and there was no end of the field in sight, Lauren made a three point turn and headed back the way she'd come. She arrived at the dirt lane leading to the barn again and stopped.

"Well, this makes no sense," she murmured, steering the car onto the packed dirt drive. Maybe she could find a farmer or someone else who could provide her with directions.

She pulled the keys from the ignition, got out of the car and shut the door. The cool morning was quiet save for the slight breeze rustling through the leaves of the trees. The leaf tips were taking on their autumn color; soon the landscape would turn into a glorious tapestry filled with shades of gold and crimson.

There wasn't a soul in sight as Lauren approached the barn. The farmer who owned the property was probably relaxing over a second cup of coffee and the Sterling Sentinel, she mused wryly. But it would be silly to have come this far and not check. Maybe the farmer was compulsive about his life's work and was inside the barn tuning his tractor or whatever it was farmers did inside of barns.

Peeling paint covered the clunky door latch, but the hinges must have been well-oiled because they swung open with silent ease.

"Hello," she called into the shadowy recesses. "Anybody here?"

She sighed and was just turning to leave when she noticed it. The shaft of light shining into the barn from the open door illuminated a steel gray tool box. Lauren frowned, one hand still bracing the tall door. Black, block-lettered decals positioned on the battered metal lid of the tool box spelled out FLYNN.

Irritation jutted Lauren's jaw as she muttered, "Dilapidated shed. Yeah, right."

One good shove opened the door fully, and then she took several more steps inside. Dust danced on thin fingers of light peeking through the slatted walls of the barn.

A wide workbench ran the length of the wall closest to her. And as her eyes became more accustomed to the dim light, she made out two metal supporting posts extending toward the ceiling. She was making a bee line for one when she caught sight of two huge, black eyes staring at her through the shadows. Lauren slapped a hand over her mouth and gasped, and at the very same moment she realized that the animal wasn't real.

She let out her pent-up breath, every muscle in her body going soft. But she'd been startled enough that when she swiped shaky fingers across her brow, they came away damp.

Curiosity drew her deeper into the barn's dusty recesses. Her lips parted in awe as she saw not one but many pairs of eyes.

A tiger. An elephant. A giraffe. A zebra. A lion. A llama. A leopard. And horses. Lots of fanciful horses.

A merry-go-round of circus animals.

Not until she stepped up onto the platform did she realize she was smiling. Broadly.

When she'd been a young girl and her mother had still been alive, her parents had taken her to the Maryland seashore every summer. There, at the boardwalk amusement park, she had ridden a merry-go-round. The gaily painted animals glided up and down, carrying her around and around to the spirited sounds of circus music. She had laughed and waved to her mom and dad with each swift revolution.

Lauren reached out and smoothed her hand over the fierce lion's mane, savoring the happy memories. Her hand came away grimy and she wiped her palm on her jeans.

Even though the brass poles and railings were dulled by tarnish and the paint on the animals was worn and chipped, the merry-go-round was amazing. She moseyed along the platform, noticing that the ride was made up of three circles. Exotic circus animals comprised the outer ring. The inner most one was made up fancy, plumed horses. The center circle consisted of fixed items—an elegant sleigh, a lavish wagon, an old jalopy, an antique fire engine.

She stepped off the platform and brushed her hands against her thighs. The entire contraption was coated with what must have been dozens of years of dirt and dust. Lauren stepped back a few feet, hands on her hips, taking in the enchanting sight.

How did it end up here? Where had it come from?

The idea that this amazing piece of machinery with its whimsical circus animals and stylish, prancing horses belonged to her—or very soon would—made her grin. The land, the shed and all its contents were hers, the judge had ruled it so.

How wonderful would it be to see this old girl cleaned up and twirling to the happy tune of an old-time Wurlitzer? Lauren reached out to stroke the giraffe's long neck but went still when she heard a noise.

Then another short, soft scuffling sound drew her gaze toward a rough-hewn door at the far side of the barn.

A barn cat, maybe? Trapped in the room and searching for a way out?

Rats? That thought sent a cold shiver shooting up her spine.

She heard a thump—if that was a rat, it was a huge one—then a muffled expletive. Whatever was behind that door, it sure wasn't a rodent.

The inclination to flee had her turning toward the door. But she hadn't taken even a single step before this odd protective instinct squared her shoulders and had her frowning. This was her land, her barn, her merry-go-round. She refused to let some vagrant or group of partying teens vandalize her property.

"I don't know who you are," she called out sternly, "but you'd better come out. Now."

The door wobbled a bit on its hinges as it was pushed open.

"Lauren?" Greg stepped out, shirtless, the top button of his jeans undone, the leather laces of his work boots loose and dragging on the dirt floor. He reached to scratch an itch on the flat of his belly. "What are you doing here?"

"What am I doing here?" she asked. "What are you doing here?" Before he could answer, she said, "You look like you just woke up."

"I was working on a project last night." He indicated the pieces of cove molding stretched out on the workbench, then he covered a yawn with his hand. "I got tired and crashed. There's a cot back there."

"Weren't you cold? It was chilly last night." For some reason, her questions sounded accusatory.

"I found a blanket." He rubbed his bare chest with his palm. "Guess I got hot in the night. Tossed my shirt somewhere. It's dark in there. Stubbed my toe before I could find my boots."

Even hazed with sleep, Greg's coal black eyes were drop-dead sexy. His rumpled dark hair invited a woman to finger-comb it into some semblance of order.

The thought made her angry. She lifted her gaze to Greg's face. "You're trespassing."

He didn't even blink. "No I'm not. Yet. I have a day or two before I have to hand over the deed."

Silence settled over them like so much barn dust. But they were both used to that by now.

Finally, she glanced over her left shoulder at the

carousel, then up into the high rafters of the barn. "A dilapidated shed, huh?" she taunted.

He didn't respond, only shook his head and disappeared into the darkness of the back room. When he returned, he was pushing his arms into the sleeves of a black t-shirt.

"When are you going to let go of the anger, Lauren?" He began tucking his shirt into the waistband at the back of his jeans.

Without missing a beat, she said, "When you admit that being married to you was no picnic for me." But the victory offered by the zinger lasted a mere nanosecond before the top of his zipper parted and his belly button flashed at her like the teasing wink of an eye. A rush of pure lust shot through her.

"I messed up," he told her. "I know it. You know it. Lew knows it. The whole town knows it, Lauren. Why can't we just move on?"

"Messed up? Is that what you call it? You lost the store, Greg."

He bent down and tied the leather laces of one boot before lifting his chin and capturing her eyes with his. "Yes. The store went under. That fact was established months ago."

He was weary of the reminder. That much was

clear from his expression. But Lauren didn't care if the truth wearied him or not.

"You lied to me. You hid things!" Ire sent blood whooshing through her ears and she welcomed it, clung to it, because anger was an emotion she knew how to handle.

Greg remained silent as he dipped his head and tied his other boot. Then he stood and just looked at her for several long seconds. He reached into his pocket and pulled out his key ring.

"Being married to you was no circus for me, either," he said before turning on his heel and heading back into the room from which he'd emerged.

"What is that supposed to mean?" she called after him.

All he said was "See you later."

Seconds later, Greg's truck engine revved to life. He must have been parked behind the barn because she hadn't seen his truck when she'd pulled onto the property. Once he'd driven away, the shadowy interior of the barn was filled with utter quiet once again.

Lauren ground her teeth and clenched her fists. The man was infuriating. The demise of their marriage had been one hundred percent his fault.

He'd hidden things from her and lied to her. His behavior had completely destroyed her trust in him. She refused to take any blame for their divorce.

Slowly she turned and let her gaze sweep across the merry-go-round. The enchantment she'd felt just minutes ago was gone. Now the thing looked old and dirty and just plain worn out. On a lark, she picked up a rag from the workbench and rubbed the brass pole that held the giraffe upright. The metal remained dull and lifeless. She rubbed some more, this time harder. Only a chemical tarnish remover could take away the years of abuse and make the brass shine again.

She took a backward step as realization struck. Surely her husband the visionary extraordinaire had good reason to keep her in the dark about this property. He had probably taken one look at the carousel and started fantasizing. In fact, he'd probably conjured some sort of wild pipe dream about opening an amusement park on Skeeter Neck Road.

Lauren tossed the rag back onto the bench as though it had caught flame and singed the skin off her fingers.

If there was one thing she knew about herself it

was that she always kept her feet firmly planted in reality. She wanted one thing from this property and one thing only—to recoup the losses she'd incurred when the store went under.

Recovering that money would allow her to set her retirement account to rights. It would also enable her to once again help her father with his rent so he could enjoy his own living space.

The thought had her glancing at her watch. She'd better get a move on or she was going to hear an earful of grumbling, that was certain. Her dad was the kind of person who would show up thirty minutes early for his own funeral. She'd agreed to meet him at ten, but when she arrived he'd probably be pacing the curb in front of his apartment building with his suitcase in hand.

Clapping the dust from her palms, Lauren felt better. Clearer headed. Grounded. She gave the animals one last look before heading for the door. There had to be somebody somewhere who was interested in purchasing an acre of ground and a ramshackle merry-go-round.

Of course there was. And she intended to find them.

* * *

She weaved through the parking lot of the Holly

Oaks apartment complex, confident that she'd be arriving right on time. Just as she expected, she saw someone at the curb. But as she got closer she realized that someone wasn't her father.

Greg had his shoulder rammed against the back of her father's ugly, green leather easy chair and he was shoving for all he was worth, trying to load it onto the back of his pick up.

"Greg," she called, slamming her car door shut and stalking toward him, "what are you doing?"

"I think—" he strained and grunted, moving the chair an inch "—that's fairly obvious."

"What are you doing here?" she clarified. He'd said not twenty minutes ago that he'd see her later, but she'd thought that was an all-around, general-purpose goodbye. "I hired some muscle. They'll be here in just a few minutes."

Again, Greg grunted and pushed. "I'll say it again." Another shove. "It's obvious what I'm doing here." After a third grunt, he said, "You want to give me a hand?"

She wasn't touching that chair. As far as she knew it was going on the curb for the Good Will pick up she'd scheduled for later.

Just then, the chair slid into the bed of the truck as if it were on wheels. He straightened and heaved a sigh. "Thanks so much," he said, his tone missing any hint of appreciation.

She tucked her keys into her back pocket. "I have guys coming, Greg. I'll have plenty of help once they arrive."

He lifted a shoulder with nonchalance. "Talk to your dad. I agreed to help because he asked." He turned away from her and reached for the length of rope sitting next to the chair leg.

Shifting her gaze toward the brick building, Lauren shook her head and grimaced. She hadn't planned for the day to go like this. What was her father thinking asking Greg to help him move? She stalked toward the front door.

The living room of the apartment was littered with cardboard boxes, some of them already taped shut, others with flaps hanging open.

"Dad," she called, closing the door behind her. "Where are you?"

"Back here."

She followed his voice toward the bedroom at the back of the unit.

"What's going on?" she asked. "Why did you ask Greg to help?"

Her dad was folding up a pair of pajama bottoms. "Because he has a truck."

"But we talked about this. I have two college students coming. One owns a truck and the other one owns a van. We'll be fine." She peeked at her watch. "They'll be here any minute."

He chuckled. "If they didn't party too hard last night."

Lauren pursed her lips. He had a point. But these young men had seemed responsible when she'd talked to them. That's why she'd hired them.

"They'll be here, Dad."

He snorted as he tucked the pants into his suitcase.

"And what about that chair? I thought we decided—"

"I need my chair. I want it."

He hadn't looked at her, not even a glance. Lauren went quiet for a moment, wondering what was really going on. "Okay," she said calmly. "If it's important to you, we'll find a place for it."

He said nothing.

"Look, today was supposed to be a good day. A fun day. Remember?" She slid her thumbs into her back pockets. "Now he's here and I just know he'll irritate the heck out of me."

Her father zipped the case with more force than

was necessary. "Could you suck it up for one blasted day?"

His bellow took her aback, knocking every last trace of wind out of her sails.

"If your boys don't show up," he continued, "we're going to need Greg. And even if they do, he's agreed to offer another pair of hands. Try to see it as a good thing, would you?"

He picked up the case and stormed out of the room, leaving her standing there all alone.

Wow. Eeyore was extra grumpy today. Then it hit her; of course, he was upset. He didn't want to leave his apartment. This had been his home for years. Sorting through his things, deciding what to keep, what to give away, had to be traumatic. He didn't want this change. Didn't want to move in with her. What seventy-year-old man wanted to give up his independence?

Guilt nipped at her for making such a fuss. About the chair. About Greg. She decided to cut her dad some slack. She'd suck it up, just as he'd asked. She'd do what she could to make this easier for him. She'd smile her way though the day. She'd get along with Greg if it killed her.

Oh, Lord, it was going to kill her.

Chapter Four

I rob banks because that's where the money is.
~Willie Sutton

"**D**o you understand the charges that have been brought against you, Mrs. Fox?" Judge Cramer was doing his best not to lose his temper.

Lauren hoped he could get a straight answer from the woman. Having spent an hour discussing the arrest and the court proceedings with her client, Lauren had come to the conclusion that the elderly woman had a rapier-sharp knack of being cunningly evasive. A retired librarian, Dorothy Fox lived in Boca Raton, Florida. She claimed to be passing through Sterling on her way to visiting all of the forty-eight contiguous United States when she was arrested for petty theft at the Town Visitor's Center where she was caught, red-handed, loading fifty-two rolls of toilet paper into the back of her station wagon.

Short and stocky, she stood silently before the judge in a long-sleeved, polyester shirt dress, belted at the waist and buttoned to the neck. Lauren fought the urge to fan herself every time she looked at the woman. Her ample bosom hung like two ripe pears that promised wide-arcing swings with any quick moves.

Judge Cramer frowned at Lauren and she offered him a small shrug.

His gaze was stern when he asked, "Ms. Fox, how do you plead?"

The woman lifted her chin, the saggy skin on her neck wobbling when she swallowed. "I plead for mercy."

Lauren rolled her eyes. "Dottie, I explained this a dozen times—"

"Your Honor, I object." The prosecutor, Harry Northrup, was obviously growing as impatient as everyone else in the courtroom.

The judge banged his gavel twice. "Hush, you two!" To the accused, he said, "You heard the police report, did you not? Is there something about the accusations that's not clear to you?"

"I don't understand why I was arrested. Everyone knows the TP in those places is free."

"The paper products offered at the Visitors Center is intended for the use of visiting tourists."

Dottie's eyes went wide and she placed her hand on her chest. "But I'm a tourist."

Lauren thought she saw wisps of steam curling from the judge's ears.

"Ms Fox, you know very well that those... supplies are to be used on the premises."

Lifting her hands, palms up, Dottie whined, "But I didn't have to go then."

Humor riffled through the courtroom spectators. The judge banged his gavel, anger turning his entire head and neck flame-red.

"She admitted to possessing the toilet paper," Harry pointed out.

The judge ignored him as he nearly shouted at the woman, "You've taken up enough of this court's time. You've delayed our entire schedule. How do you plead?"

"Well, my lawyer said we would have to throw ourselves on the mercy of the court. But... well—"

she rested one hand on her ample hip "—I'm too old and feeble to be throwing myself anywhere."

She might be old, Lauren surmised, but she was about as feeble as a Brahma bull. Judge Cramer cracked the gavel to subdue the new, and this time blatant, surge of laughter from the audience.

"I've explained this three times already, Ms. Fox!"

Lauren thought the man's head was going to explode. Harry scrubbed his face with both his hands.

"You've been accused of petty theft." He enunciated the words as if he were speaking to an imbecile. "You must plead. You do not, however, have to plead guilty. If you plead not guilty, then you must return to Sterling to stand trial when a court date is set."

"But, see," Dottie said, completely unruffled by the judge's angry tone, "that won't work for me. I'm on a quest. I'm driving to each—"

"Yes, yes," Judge Cramer said. "You've already told us about that. So do you want to plead guilty?"

"But I didn't do anything wrong. Everyone knows that if you need toilet paper you go to a public restroom."

Cramer looked like he was about to pass out.

"Your Honor, may I speak?" Lauren asked, fearing his volcanic wrath might finally erupt and spew a contempt charge all over her and her client. "I explained to Ms. Fox, numerous times, how the court works. We went over the scenario of her pleading not guilty, and how the court would then set a date for her trial. Then bail would be set at somewhere around two hundred fifty dollars. Cash. I told her she'd then be free to go. She could drive away, visit another state or two, while she thinks about this matter. I also explained that she could come back to change her plea at any time before the trial begins."

Two hundred fifty dollars was the normal fine charged by the county for petty theft. No one in their right mind would expect this scheming little old lady to return to the Sterling to stand trial. If she were released, she'd drive out of Maryland like a NASCAR favorite, never to be seen again.

Lauren had been in this business long enough to peg a con artist a mile away. She had realized it from the moment Dottie Fox had walked into her office. She'd agreed to offer her services if, and only if, she was paid up front and in cash. And Dottie had a wad of dough tucked between those pears of hers.

The woman was guilty as sin. If Dottie pled guilty, she'd be fined and sent on her way. If she pled not guilty, she'd be set free on bail; and if she didn't return to court for her hearing, the county would receive its due in the form of the forfeited bail money. But the woman had to plead one way or the other in order for the case to move forward, and this fiasco had already been going on for far too long. A cluster of lawyers and their clients were slowly filling the back of the courtroom, their cases waiting to be heard.

"So is that what you want to do, Ms. Fox?" the judge asked. "You want to plead not guilty?"

"Well—" she blinked several times, an innocent look shifting the wrinkles on her face "—can I go with my original idea and just plead for mercy?"

The whole courtroom wrenched with a collective groan.

* * *

Twilight glowed through her office window, giving the tawny paint on the walls a pinkish hue. The five-inch-thick tome spread-eagled on Lauren's desk captured every nuance of her attention as she studied Maryland case law for an upcoming court appearance.

The desk light snapped on, startling her into sitting up straight.

"You're going to go blind," Norma Jean warned.

"Thanks." Lauren took in the woman's jacket and scarf. "You heading out?"

Norma nodded. "I finished up the filing so I'm going home for some dinner. If you're going to be here much longer, you should go next door and grab something to eat."

"Right. Dinner." The springs of her chair squeaked as she pushed away from her desk. "My dad's home alone." She sighed. "I've got another hour of reading to do, but I guess I should go home."

Lauren stood and stretched. Then she yawned.

"Tough day." Norma shifted the stylish scarf hugging her neck.

"Frustrating, mostly."

Judge Cramer had finally wrestled a not guilty plea from Dottie Fox. The woman posted bail and walked out of the courthouse. Lauren expected the elderly lady to make a wide berth around the entire state of Maryland for the rest of her life. And the state wouldn't go looking for her. Chasing down petty criminals would cost tax payers too much money, especially since the court would eventually claim the cash Dottie had been forced to leave with the court clerk for bail.

"How are things going with your dad?" Norma Jean asked.

Lauren shrugged. "Not bad. It's only been a few days, of course. One thing is certain; I sure did take my privacy for granted. It's small things, really. Taking a bath, for instance. I used to soak in a hot tub with a glass of wine for as long as I wanted without giving it a thought. But now I can't seem to relax enough to enjoy it."

Norma's head tilted in commiseration. "I'm sure that will change in time."

"And the dinner thing," Lauren said. "I haven't cooked in... I can't tell you how long. Now I feel like I have to plan meals and go to the grocery store." She shook her head. "I've never been the homemaker type."

The pink shadows on the walls were quickly deepening to mauve.

"Look, Lauren, I go right by your house on my way home." Norma hitched the leather strap of her big, fashionable handbag higher on her shoulder. "If you've got work to do, I could pick up a sandwich from Nick's next door and take it to your dad."

Nick's Deli was a favored watering hole for both women.

A mixture of relief and gratitude rounded Lauren's shoulders. "That would be great, Norma Jean. You're sure you don't mind?"

The woman waved off her concern. "I'd love to. I haven't seen your dad in ages."

Snatching up her purse, Lauren dug out a twenty and handed it over. "I appreciate this so much."

"Don't even think about," Norma said, tucking the bill into her jacket pocket and turning toward the door. "Night."

"See you tomorrow."

An hour or so later, Lauren leaned away from her computer and rubbed her eyes. She'd gone from combing through several volumes in her meager library to researching the myriad public records on-line. She should go home. The long day had exhausted her. But rather than packing up her files, she reached toward the keyboard and typed the URL of her favorite search engine.

MERRY-GO-ROUND, she tapped the keywords and clicked 'search.'

The offerings were overwhelming. Amusement parks, circus museums, clown blogs, images galore.

She even saw several YouTube hits. But none of the links were exactly what she was looking for, so she tried again.

MERRY-GO-ROUND FOR SALE. She hit the enter key and waited.

She was amazed to discover websites that acted like huge used car lots, only they sold second-hand amusement park rides. Who bought this stuff?

Scanning the site, she found her answer; shopping malls, family entertainment centers, traveling carnivals.

But all of these places would want the merry-go-round to come to them. Lauren wanted a buyer to come to her merry-go-round. Because she had an acre of ground to go with the ride.

She sat back, resting her fists on the edge of her desk. She didn't even know if the carousel worked. And all of these rides offered for sale were clean, their brass polished, their paint bright. It would be difficult enough to sell a piece of land out on Skeeter Neck Road; it would be impossible if it came with a dirty, worn, broken down carnival ride.

Those fancy circus horses pranced through her brain. What little girl wouldn't want one of those beauties in her bedroom?

Of course, that would mean dismantling the merry-go-round and turning the faded, grimy horses into beauties. But that could be done with a little elbow grease and paint, couldn't it?

Her fingers flew as she punched in the keywords. CAROUSEL HORSES FOR SALE.

Jackpot!

There was a market for her horses. And the other animals, too. Then she gawked when she saw the price of some of them. They were being advertised at upwards of ten thousand dollars or more. She leaned forward, looked closer. Each.

Her heart pounded like a fist against her ribs. There must be twenty or thirty animals on that thing. Maybe more. She hadn't taken the time to count them. She could become solvent again. She could recoup her losses and then some; she did a quick, mental calculation. Some? She could stand to gain nearly a quarter of a million dollars. And that wasn't counting the acre of land. Good mercy, Ms. Percy!

She shoved her chair out into the middle of the floor and spun around in a circle, grinning like a monkey. A monkey that had just discovered a hidden treasure.

Suddenly she sobered. She really couldn't do

anything until she had the deed in hand. When they'd moved her father on Saturday, Greg had promised to have it to her by Wednesday. Tomorrow she'd be a rich woman. Her chuckle reverberated off the walls of her office. Okay, nowhere near rich, maybe, but wealthier than she was today.

An odd, dark emotion poked at her. Should she tell Greg? Did he know what he'd lost when the judge had taken the land from him? Lauren doubted it.

Should she share the money with him?

She slid her palms up and down her thighs.

Legally, she had every right to keep whatever profits she earned from selling what was rightfully hers. But what were the ethical aspects of the situation?

The man had no financial acumen whatsoever. He'd cost her a ton of money. Not to mention months and months of stress.

She deserved this as payment for all her pain and suffering, didn't she?

Yes, she did.

Lauren slid back to her desk and powered down her computer. Then she got up and started stuffing files into her briefcase, unable to shake the feeling that she was doing something wrong.

She deserved this, she heard her ego whisper again.

She shouldn't worry about this any more. Greg had made his bed of nails; let him lie on it. She'd done everything she had been legally obligated to do. She was going to put it out of her head. In fact, she was going to go home, submerge herself in a steamy bath and enjoy a glass of wine.

"I deserve this," she said firmly as she flipped off the light in her office.

So why did she feel like Dottie Fox with her station wagon full of toilet paper?

Chapter Five

Ah, yes, divorce. . .from the Latin word
meaning to rip out a man's genitals
through his wallet.
~Robin Williams

"**I**'m off to work, Dad," Lauren called as she headed toward the kitchen. "Have a good day." Bright sunshine set the room aglow. She pulled up short when she saw her father.

"More coffee?" she asked. "You think you should have more caffeine? You know how it affects you."

"As long as I don't drink any after noon, I'm fine. I want another cup of coffee." He finished pouring a full pot of water into the reservoir without looking at her.

"Another cup?"

"Don't mother hen me, Lauren." He set the glass carafe on the burner, flipped on the switch and then turned to face her.

"Okay, okay," she said, backing off, even though she figured he'd probably call her this afternoon complaining that he'd developed a mean case of tinnitus.

They'd been house buddies for nearly a week now, and she was doing her best to get along with him.

"Have fun today." She reached up and gave him a quick kiss on the cheek.

"You, too." He glanced at the clock on the stove. "Hadn't you better get a move on? You're going to be late." He reached for the newspaper sitting on the counter and headed for a sunny spot at the kitchen table.

She waggled her fingers at him as she left the room. On her way to the front door she stopped by the hall table and picked up the mail that had been piling there for a couple days. She stuffed it into the side pocket of her briefcase and locked the front door behind her.

Twisting to watch where she was going, she backed the car out of the drive way, her mind focused on the appointments that were lined up for her today. Two new clients were coming in this morning. And she would spend a better part of the afternoon in court. Then she had an intimidating letter to write on a client's behalf; sometimes a well-worded threat to sue provoked action and saved time and money for the people she worked for.

By the time she'd registered that she'd seen Greg, he'd already passed her on his way, she guessed, to her house. She glanced at the rearview mirror and watched him pull into the driveway.

No wonder her dad was making a pot of coffee rather than just a cup. She thought it odd though that, if he had been expecting Greg to come for a visit, why hadn't he just said so? Why hide it?

It wasn't as if she expected her father to stop speaking to Greg because she was divorcing the man. But maybe he thought she'd be upset at the thought of Greg visiting him at the house? Maybe he, too, was doing his best to keep the peace now that they were living under the same roof.

Snapping on the radio, she listened to the

national news for the few minutes it took to drive to the office.

The deadbolt on the door thunked as she turned the key. She opened the blinds on the large front window and turned up the thermostat to take the autumn chill out of the air. She usually arrived at the office before Norma Jean because she liked to spend a few minutes getting settled before the phones started ringing and clients arrived.

After plugging in the electric kettle and plopping a tea bag into a mug, she went into her office and sat at her desk. She sorted through the mail she'd pulled from her briefcase. Bills and correspondence in one pile, sales brochures and other junk mail headed for the garbage can in another.

The large, white envelope was tucked between a couple of thick sales flyers. The return address on the front made her heart skitter. She ripped into it like a child with a long-awaited, gaily-wrapped birthday present.

She grasped the document inside the envelope, slowly pulled it into the light of day, placed it in front of her with something akin to reverence and leaned back. The official decree sat on the desk top, and she just stared.

It was official. She was a divorced woman. She was free. She was single.

An odd feeling swept over her.

Before the papers had arrived, she had imagined this moment many times over. In fact, imagining this moment had gotten her through some of the roughest times over the past year or so. She had envisioned herself running to the liquor store to buy a bottle of expensive champagne. She'd fantasized about celebrating her divorce by painting Sterling bright red, drinking and dancing from one hot spot to another, showing everyone the papers that made her a free woman.

But she simply sat and stared.

What was wrong with her? She'd thought once her ties to Greg had been well and truly severed she'd feel as if a huge weight had been lifted off her. She had thought she would feel... lighter... happier... *something*.

But she felt nothing.

No, not nothing. There was emotion churning behind her solar plexus. But what was it exactly?

The whistling kettle had her on her feet and padding to the office's small efficiency kitchen. She poured steaming water over the tea bag and watched it turn a golden brown.

She should be snapping her fingers, swiveling her hips and dancing the jitterbug around her desk. Not that she knew how to jitterbug. She would if she'd let her parents teach her when they'd wanted to all those years ago; however, she'd been content to sit on the staircase and watch through the railings while they twisted and shook and swung each other around the living room floor.

Lauren contemplatively stirred honey into her tea.

Divorce wasn't something to be taken lightly. And she hadn't.

She and Greg had shared some wonderful times. But the final year they'd been together had shown such a bright light on their differences that she could no longer avoid seeing them.

She carried her mug back into her office and settled at her desk.

Separating herself from him had been the right thing to do. For her, at least.

He'd fought her tooth and nail. He'd suggested a host of remedies: a romantic vacation (who could afford to fly off to the Bahamas when a business was going under?), separate bank accounts (too late), counseling (no way was she going to chance some professional talking her into seeing Greg's point of view).

During those last months of the marriage, she'd felt as if she'd been swept up into some financial whirlpool that would surely suck her bank account and her bones completely dry. And that was nearly what had happened. Not only that, but before it was all over her emotions had been as spent as her checking account.

Every time she thought about what had happened, she became so ticked off she could barely speak, and that anger overrode everything else. Even the strange, heavy feeling that sprouted in the pit of her belly right now upon seeing the official divorce papers. She set down the mug with more force than she meant to. Tea sloshed onto the postcard advertisement for a local pizza joint and one, wide corner of a white, business-size envelope sticking out from beneath the unsorted pile of mail.

Lauren tossed the postcard into the wire wastebasket, and then reached for the envelope, grabbing a tissue from the box on her desk at the same time. As she blotted off the worst of the mess, she noticed Greg's name neatly printed in the upper left corner.

She slid her thumbnail under the flap and ripped the paper with short, jerky tugs. The deed to the Skeeter Neck property was tucked inside. Lauren placed the document next to the divorce decree.

The front door of the office whispered open and she heaved a deep breath.

"Morning," she called out to Norma Jean. "I'm glad you're here. I need to talk about the vast contradiction of good and evil sitting on my desk."

She got up, grinning at her joke, and made for the door leading to the reception area... where she nearly bumped into a good-looking, sandy-haired, blue-eyed man.

He reached out and grasped her shoulders so their forward momentum didn't cause them to collide. "Sorry," he murmured.

"I was expecting Norma Jean." The quick start and stop had dislodged a tendril of her hair from the twist she'd hastily pinned up this morning. "My receptionist," she clarified, swiping the lock back from where it had fallen across her cheek.

Lauren glanced at her watch.

"Yes, yes," the man rushed to say. "I'm early. I called, but couldn't reach anyone. I did leave a message."

Automatically, she peeked around him and saw

the red blinking light on the telephone-slash-answering machine-slash-intercom that sat on Norma's desk.

"I hope I'm not messing up your day," he told her.

Taking a backward step, Lauren smiled. "Of course not."

His amazing, blue eyes were the first thing she noticed. He was tall. At least six foot. The black business suit fitted his body well. And his eyes were vivid blue. She'd describe him as trim and athletic-looking rather than bulkily muscular. A long distance runner, maybe? *And those eyes...* They were enough to make a woman's thoughts go haywire.

She thrust out her hand automatically. "Lauren Flynn."

He shook it, smiling, and that gaze of his twinkled.

"Scott Shaw. I'm Scotty's father."

Lauren nodded. "Ah, yes. Scott. He called and said he wanted me to represent him."

When the man automatically reached for the pocket on the inside of his suit jacket, she told him, "Come on in." She retreated behind her desk, but didn't sit. "Can I get you something? Coffee? Tea?"

"No, thanks. I've got appointments this morning."

He handed her a check and she couldn't help but notice what neat penmanship he had.

"Scotty would have brought this himself, but he had class this morning." His jaw firmed and so did his tone. "He's going to be focusing on his grades more and partying less. And he'll be keeping his nose clean. That much I can assure anyone who's interested. The police. A judge. The Dean. You."

Uh-oh. Sounds like poor Scott, Jr. wasn't in just a bit of hot water with his father, he was in a tub full.

"You don't have to worry about me," she assured him. She set the check on her desk. "I'm on his side."

"And we appreciate that, too. Very much." He tucked his checkbook back into his jacket. "Can you tell me what to expect? When Scotty goes to court, I mean?"

"Well, I can promise you that your son will get a firm lecture from the judge." She crossed her arms. "I'm sure he'll be fined. And depending on who oversees the case, he could get some probation. However, I will do everything I can to keep his punishment to a minimum."

The man nodded, his serious gaze never leaving her face. He made her feel as if she were the only person alive at that particular moment.

"It's not the court's intention to ruin Scott's life over this." She let her hands fall to her sides.

"Yes." He sighed. "They just want to ram home the message that stupid behavior has consequences."

"Exactly." She reached out and touched the check he'd written. "I'll need your signature on the retainer agreement."

"I'd like for my son to sign any formal documents, if you don't mind. He'll be footing one hundred percent of the bill for this little escapade. That—" he pointed to the check "—is just a loan."

When Scott, Jr. had told her that he had no job and that he was given a weekly allowance, she'd pegged him as spoiled and his father as a pushover.

"I didn't mind providing a free ride as long as he was acting like he had some sense. But now... " He lifted one shoulder. "Gainful employment is in my son's immediate future. I'm paying the retainer because I want him to have solid representation, but I expect him to repay every nickel. And he'll be responsible for any fees over that, as well."

Wow. The man was quickly proving himself anything but a pushover.

"But don't worry," he said, his blue eyes glittering. "If something happens, if he can't find a job or packs his bags and flees the state before his court date, I won't let him stiff you."

She grinned.

He shifted his weight on his feet, looking at her desk. She thought he was staring at the check he'd given her and she wondered if he might be having second thoughts about loaning his son the retainer fee.

Softly, he asked, "So, are congratulations in order?"

"Excuse me?"

Scott chuckled, pointing. "I know finalized divorce papers when I see them. If they belonged to one of your clients, the state wouldn't have sent them here."

Her gaze unwittingly fell on the decree; then one corner of her mouth lifted. "That's true. And I'm guilty as charged."

He smiled, and those gorgeous eyes flashed. "So congratulations are in order."

Lauren continued to smile at him, not certain how to respond.

"And I see that, like my ex, you're a good house keeper."

Her smile slipped. Then she saw what he was looking at. She picked up the deed, chuckling at his joke. "Oh, this isn't for the house." She found she was blushing as she explained, "I did keep the house. But that was only fair since it was mine before we got married."

His brows arched. "A fair-minded woman? Wow. Wish I'd been that lucky. My wife kept our house, our SUV, half the savings and—drum roll, please—half my pension."

"Ouch!" Lauren winced.

He sighed. "Yeah, she sold the house within a year and moved to Atlanta. An up and coming city full of opportunity, she called it. She's remarried now, and raising kids that are his and theirs, and she rarely calls our son."

She'd grown used to listening to people's woes. For some reason, the public seemed to look at lawyers as they did psychiatrists or counselors; the money you offer for services includes an ear to bend and a shoulder to lean on.

"That woman is a piece of work, I don't mind saying. Scotty flies down there to spend a week with his mother every summer." Scott Shaw's mouth flattened, then he added, "Whether he wants to or not."

Lauren found herself nodding.

His head cocked slightly as he looked at her askance. "You look like you just put two and two together and came up with four."

The smile she offered was evasive. "Just making sense of something your son said when he was here."

It's just my dad, the young man had told her when she'd mentioned his parents. For the most part. Now she understood. Before he could inquire further, she said, "You're sure I can't get you something?"

"No. Really. I have to go." He backed through her office door as he spoke and she followed him out into the reception area.

Norma Jean pulled open the front door and called out, "Hello, hello!"

After shooting Norma a smile and a tipped-chin greeting, Scott Shaw turned back to Lauren. "When you meet with Scotty to go over things, would it be all right if I came along with him?"

"Sure. If it's okay with your son, it's okay with me."

He went still suddenly. "And, uh, maybe I could

take you to lunch some day. You know—" he grinned wickedly "—to celebrate."

The invitation was so unexpected she couldn't think of a single thing to say or do. Her mouth widened of its own accord, and she saw her hands lifted outward even though she hadn't given conscious thought to the action.

"Maybe." She croaked the word rather than spoke it.

He winked at her. "I hope you'll take me up on the offer. It'll be fun." He moved to the front door. "I'll see you soon."

After nodding goodbye to Norma Jean, Scott waltzed out the door.

"Who was that?"

Lauren turned her attention to Norma, feeling for the first time in many minutes that she could take a nice, deep breath.

"Mr. Shaw," she said. "Scott Shaw's father."

"The Shaw appointment wasn't until nine-thirty."

Lauren nodded. "He said he tried to call."

"He brought the retainer? We've got a new client?" She made her way to the front of the office, to the big picture window. "Great. I'll work up a file."

But it was clear her mind wasn't on office procedure at the moment. She was too busy watching the man cross the street.

"You going to go? To lunch, I mean? I think you should, Lauren." She gave a little wolf whistle. "Oh, yes, I think you should."

"What's that you brought?" Lauren asked, hoping to change the subject.

Norma Jean glanced at the covered dish she'd set on her desk but didn't move from her spot. "Oh, I made a casserole. For Lew's dinner tonight."

"Well, thanks. That was awfully nice."

"Actually, I thought I'd follow you home. We could all eat together. There's plenty there." She busied herself unbuttoning and then slipping off her jacket, her eyes still trained out the window. "I had a good time talking with him the other night."

"Sure," Lauren said. "Dinner at my place sounds great. I'll pick up a bottle of wine at lunch. I'll put the casserole in the fridge for you."

She reached over and picked up the dish, but Norma Jean came over, caught one of the handles and met her gaze levelly.

"So... you going to go?"

"Probably not," Lauren said. "I don't even know the man."

Norma let go and walked to the front door. "You should. That is one heavenly piece of man meat."

Lauren just shook her head. "Would you come away from there? He's going to catch you staring."

She hoped she would be as zesty as Norma was when she reached her sixties.

"No harm in looking." Her nose was nearly pressed to the glass. "Did you see those eyes?"

Turning on her heel, Lauren headed for the break room refrigerator as she asked, "He had eyes?"

She wasn't surprised that her glib remark prompted no response. Norma was too busy studying the man meat.

Chapter Six

I beg your pardon;
I was not in the rear of the barn.
I was in the other end of the barn
that faced the street.
~Lizzie Andrew Borden

For the third day in a row, Lauren left the house in a hurry. More like, she'd been shooed out by her father. It was as if the man couldn't wait for her to get out of the door each morning so he could read the paper in peace or turn on his laptop and start surfing the Net.

As she pulled out of her neighborhood, Greg was once again pulling in. He offered a quick smile and lifted his hand in greeting, but he passed by before she had time to react.

The frown between her brows bit deeper the farther she drove away from home. Was this the third time she'd passed Greg on his way to her house over the past week, or the fourth? She tilted her head just a fraction. Could it really be the fifth?

Who her father visited with was no business of hers. Lauren tried to focus on the day ahead, plan out the phone calls she had to make, the people she needed to see, but her thoughts of work soon scattered.

She knew her dad and her ex were close, but five visits in a week? That just didn't make sense.

Men didn't normally participate in coffee klatches. They didn't sit over crullers and hazelnut lattes, dishing the dirt like women did.

Or did they?

"Noooo." She whispered the answer, shaking her head and chuckling as she drew the small word out.

Men didn't talk. Not about anything meaningful, anyway. They watched football on TV and discussed the players' stats. They visited home improvement stores and pointed out the items on their wish lists. They scratched itches and shifted private parts in public. No way were they social enough to participate in civilized, chatty conversation.

Lauren grinned as she turned onto South Avenue and entered town. She wasn't being fair and she knew it. She oughtn't to think that way about fifty one point four percent of the human race.

Something seemed fishy, though. Five visits in a week. That frown was back, pinching the space between her eyebrows, and a band of tension tightened with enough force to trigger the first inkling of a headache.

She circled the block, flipping open her cell and punching in Norma Jean's number to tell her she was going to be late. Lauren tossed the phone onto the passenger seat and headed out of town the way she'd come.

Greg's pick-up sat in the drive. She parked behind it. Drywall and crown molding filled the truck bed.

"Dad?" she called as she entered the foyer. "Greg?" Her heels clicked on the hardwood of the hallway as she checked the rooms in the front of the house. The kitchen was empty, too. She looked out the window and scanned the backyard, making a mental note to rake the leaves that littered the lawn.

Water was running somewhere and she climbed the stairs, tracking the sound to the main bathroom. The door was open a crack and the shower was running.

Lauren found it odd that her dad would decide to take a shower while he had a visitor. And where was Greg, anyway? Before the question had fully registered in her mind, the shower cut off.

"Dad?" She waited, and when she didn't get an answer, she knocked.

Just as it dawned on her that her father might not be the person taking the shower, she took a small backward step and the door was pulled open wide.

Hazy steam billowed into the hallway, and there stood Greg, his slick, wet body wrapped in a towel from the waist down. "Lew's not here."

"What are you doing?" Her tone reflected her utter astonishment.

He opened his mouth, but he didn't reply. A fat droplet hovered on his chin. His dark lashes were stuck together, and water ran in rivulets down his neck, shoulders and chest.

"Getting ready to shave?" He looked guilty, as if

he'd been caught with, not one, but both hands in the cookie jar.

"This isn't Jeopardy, Greg. You don't have to pose your answers in the form of a question."

Then it registered—the warm, clean scent of him. Blood whooshed through her ears, and she had to fight the urge to close her eyes and inhale deeply. Suddenly, she felt as if she were standing in a pool of bright sunlight, heat permeating every inch of her.

She blinked and swallowed and took another backward step all at the same time. "Get dressed and come down stairs. We need to talk." She headed down the hall.

"But, hold on. Wait. I can't."

Lauren stopped, curious to know what he meant; however, she came face to face with her dad who was trudging up the steps.

"Where were you? And why is he in your shower?" She pointed to her ex with a jerk of her thumb.

She looked from one man to the other.

"If you must know," her dad blustered, "I was in the basement putting in a load of laundry."

"But I took care of your laundry yesterday, Dad. If you're doing a small load, you set the water level on low, didn't you?" She looked at Greg. She rested her closed fist on her hip. "Why are you still standing there? Put on your pants and come downstairs."

Greg's dark eyes shifted from her to her dad and then back again. His expression fell as he softly admitted, "I don't have any pants up here, Lauren."

The steam in the bathroom had dissipated completely. He stood half in, half out of the doorway. The smattering of dark curls on his chest was damp, so were the curls on the flat of his belly just above the terry towel loosely tucked around his hips. A small puddle had formed around each foot, one on the hardwood hallway floor, one on the bathroom tile.

She went completely still and heat rushed through her entire body. Then she turned to her father. "You're doing his laundry." It wasn't a question.

Something weird was going on inside her. Greg's state of undress incited a dark neediness low in her gut, but it was all tangled up with the annoyance she felt when she'd finally figured out what was going on here. She was hot. In more ways than one. The only way to handle willful lust was to pay it no heed and refocus, so she grabbed hold of the aggravation with both hands and used it as a shield.

Her ex was taking a shower in her bathroom, using her towels and the hot water she paid for, and her father was washing Greg's clothes in her washing machine.

Looking at Greg was too dangerous, so she focused on her father.

"I can't even get you to do your own laundry," she said. "What would compel you to do his?"

"I can do my own wash, thank you very much" he told her. "It's just that you won't give me a chance. Stay out of my room, out of my hamper, and I'll do for myself when the need arises."

"That's a deal." She walked back down the hallway toward Greg, keeping her gaze directed at the floor as she passed by him. She pushed open her bedroom door hard enough to make it thud into the door stop, snatched up her robe from the arm of the chair, then turned around and headed back out the door.

"Put this on." She dropped the robe across Greg's outstretched arm, keeping her eyes trained on the baseboard, where the wall met the floor. "I'll see you in the kitchen."

Her dad had come up the stairs and now stood in

the hall. She brushed past him and said, "You, too, Dad."

She heard the bathroom door close on her way downstairs. Letting her hand trail along the railing, she closed her eyes, breathed deep and tried to cool the chaotic heat agitating in her. Anger, resentment, irritation, those were the things she needed to concentrate on. The other stuff, she quickly decided, didn't even exist as long as she chose to ignore it. And ignore it, she would.

In the kitchen, she dropped her keys on the counter and snatched up an orange from the wooden bowl. Not because she was hungry but because she needed something to occupy her hands so she couldn't strangle someone. She passed the orange from one palm to the other.

"This is my fault, Lauren," her dad said when he came into the kitchen. "I didn't actually tell him you knew he was coming. I didn't say this was okay with you, but, well—" the crown of his head tilted from left to right and his silver hair did a little flop "—I may have given him that impression."

"Dad, what were you thinking?" Before he could answer, she said, "Why would this ever be okay with me? Greg and I are divorced. He doesn't live here anymore. We're living completely separate lives. We have been for over a year."

His hazel eyes went dark. "I know that, Lauren. The man is a little down on his luck at the moment. I was just trying to help him out. I was only trying to do something nice. You remember what that is, don't you?"

"Give me a break." She dug her thumbnail into the orange and began peeling the skin from the flesh.

Greg came into the room looking downright silly in her russet satin robe. The hem hit him mid thigh and the knot he'd tied in the sash rested several inches above his waist.

Memories flooded her mind. Two years ago, Greg had donned her robe and served her breakfast in bed. French toast with butter and maple syrup, sliced strawberries dusted with powered sugar, coffee and juice. He'd placed a long-stemmed rose across the plate. She'd been dreading her birthday, dreading the idea of getting older. He'd shimmied around the room in that too-small robe while she ate, acting ridiculous to lift her spirits and make her laugh. And laugh is exactly what she had done.

However, Lauren was too exasperated to even

smile right now let alone laugh. And frustration had come along to fuel the fire. How could she be angry with Greg now that she knew he thought she was aware of what was going on? And what was going on, anyway?

She set the half-peeled orange aside and went to the sink to rinse her fingers. Picking up the tea towel, she slowly and methodically dried her hands. "Greg, why are you showering in my house? Doing your laundry in my laundry room?"

Having your laundry done for you, she wanted to correct, but didn't.

Then her father's words reverberated in her mind.

The man is a little down on his luck.

She groaned. "Oh, please tell me you're having plumbing problems at your apartment. Tell me a plumber's there right now. Tell me that the water company is flushing the lines and you can't use your shower today."

Greg just stood there looking at her.

Lauren sighed. "You were evicted, weren't you? When will you learn that you have to pay your bills on time? When you don't pay your rent, you get tossed out on your butt." Again she shook her head, this time with a little more fervor. "Well, you cannot stay here."

He continued to stare, not saying a word and looking as if he'd rather be anywhere in world but standing there wearing that robe.

"Would you give the man a little credit," her father grumbled. "He didn't forget to pay his bills. His water wasn't shut off, and he wasn't evicted."

Her dad crossed the kitchen. "How 'bout a cup of coffee, Greg? It's fresh." He picked up the carafe and filled his mug.

"Thanks, Lew." Greg kept his eyes leveled on Lauren. "But I think I should go gather up my things and go."

Lauren stared at him for a second or two, then she let go of the tension she was holding in her shoulders. Hadn't she told herself she wasn't going to let this man affect her any longer?

"You may as well sit down and have some coffee," she told him. She picked up the orange and began tugging at the peel again. "There's no possible way you're going to make a dignified exit looking like that."

He hesitated only a moment before nodding a response and reaching up to comb his fingers through his damp hair. He pulled out a chair and sat down at the table.

Her father took a clean cup from the dish drainer, poured coffee into it and set it on the table in front of Greg.

"Thanks, Lew."

"Welcome." Her dad filled his cup and sat down, too.

Both men seemed content to sit and sip coffee in companionable silence.

"Well, is someone going to explain what's going on?" she blustered. "If you paid your bills on time, if your water hasn't been cut off, why—"

"I gave up the apartment back in the summer."

"I don't understand." The scent of orange essence hung in the air. "You gave it up?"

He nodded and then lifted the ceramic mug to his mouth.

"But why would you do something like that?" Then a large piece of orange skin hit the kitchen floor. "You're living in that barn."

Greg studied his coffee mug, refusing to meet her gaze.

"You can't live out there. That place is filthy." Once again, she set the orange on the counter. "It's a barn, Greg. It was not meant for human habitation."

That little colloquy sounded too much like concern for her comfort.

"Besides that," she quickly added, "it's my barn."

"Well, crap," her father muttered. "Here we go."

"What?" She eyed her dad. "It is my barn."

"No one is disputing that, Lauren." Greg's tone was mollifying.

But she didn't want to be mollified. "You lied to me again. I caught you in that barn and you never said you were living there. You never said that."

His chin tipped up a fraction. "I said I was working late. Which I was. I said I fell asleep there. Which I did. I spoke nothing but the truth."

"It was a half-truth," she pointed out. "Half-truths, omissions, evasions. That's all I ever get from you, Greg." Her father's disapproving expression was like sandpaper on rash-ridden skin. "And what are you looking at? You're no better. Inviting people in to my home without telling me—"

"He'd been showering at my place. And this is my place now, too, right?"

A small gasp escaped from her throat. "He's been using my hot water since you moved in?"

"You wouldn't even know about it if you'd leave for work on time."

"Please, please, stop," Greg said. "I feel bad enough already. I don't want the two of you fighting because of me."

She clamped her mouth shut. As much as she hated to admit it, Greg was right. She shouldn't fight with her father. Arguing with him would do no good. It never had. He was going to do what he wanted. Befriend whom he wanted. Invite over whomever he wanted. Offer laundry services to the whole neighborhood. Her opinion didn't matter a wit.

Lauren went to the table, pulled out a chair and sat. "Is business that bad, Greg?" A silent groan rose up inside her at her next thought. She tried for the span of several heartbeats to hold her tongue, to keep her curiosity at bay, but in the end she just let it rip. "Do you need some money?"

She tried to make the offer sound gracious, but she missed the mark by a very wide margin. In reality, voicing the question about killed her. Giving Greg any more of her hard-earned cash was the last thing she wanted to do. But she wouldn't have been able to live with the guilt of not asking.

Why was it her responsibility to take care of everyone? Solve everyone's problems?

Her ex-husband reached out and covered her hand with his. "I'm okay, Lauren. You don't need to worry about me."

She pulled her arm back as if his touch burned. "I'm not worried." She stood then, and retreated to her spot near the counter.

Her father expressed his disbelief with a small tick of his tongue; Lauren turned a deaf ear. She rested the small of her back against the edge of the counter and crossed her arms over her chest.

"Look, Lauren," Greg said. "I'm looking for another place, okay? If you'll just let me stay out there for a—"

"No, Greg."

"Lau-ren." Disgust and disappointment weighed down the two syllables when her father spoke them. "The man isn't asking for the world."

"It's a barn, Dad," she reminded him.

Greg smiled. "Actually, it's not all that bad. I slapped up some dry wall in the back room, and I have a space heater. And there's a well. I've been carrying water in from the hand pump out back."

The primitiveness of it sent a shiver up her spine. "But there's no, you know... plumbing."

Her dad must have sensed that she was softening to the idea of Greg staying at the barn because he chuckled. "Haven't you heard, Lauren? Real men pee in the woods."

Lauren just closed her eyes.

With his I'm okay line, Greg intimated that he was earning an adequate living. But who knew how much or how little truth his veiled intimations held? He'd lied to her before. Man, oh, man, had he ever. And she couldn't fathom any other reason for him to live in that dusty, drafty old building out on swampy Skeeter Neck Road unless he had no money.

The idea that Greg needed some income forced her thoughts to make a sharp turn.

The whimsical treasure housed in that barn would be worth a small fortune, but it wasn't worth squat in its current condition. Greg was an expert carpenter; he could build just about anything. Her father once commented that Greg had 'hands.' The meaning behind the observation had become clear any time Greg had taken on a project in the house during their marriage. He could fix almost anything and he had, too, from a hole in the wall, to leaky plumbing, to a short in the electrical system. He was a true and talented Jack-of-all-trades.

And he would be the perfect person to restore those carrousel animals for her.

She looked at her ex. "You need a job?"

His dark eyes narrowed the tiniest fraction before he shook his head. "I've got plenty of work."

Lauren couldn't tell if he was being honest or if his male pride was talking.

"Okay," she said, "let me rephrase that. Would you like a job?"

"I don't know. What do you have in mind?" His question and his expression reeked of suspicion.

She reached for the orange and began removing the last bit of skin. "I'd like the merry-go-round cleaned up."

"Wow." The tension on his face relaxed and he sat back, genuinely astonished. "I have to admit, I'm surprised. I thought you'd take one look at her, have her dismantled and carted to the land fill."

"I'll pay you an hourly wage," she offered. Then she shrugged. "And if you're staying at the barn, you can work off the rent."

"Rent?" He laughed outright at the idea. "You said the place isn't fit for human habitation, and now you want to charge me rent?"

She set the orange down. "You said you fixed it up. That it was nice."

"I said it wasn't bad."

That was what he said. And the man did have to relieve himself in the woods. Thinking about his living conditions made her want to cringe all over again.

"All right. All right. No rent." She picked her keys up from where she'd tossed them on the counter. "So you'll get those animals cleaned up and painted?"

Greg nodded. "It'll take some time, though. And I'm still surprised you want it done."

She shrugged and offered him a smile. "I can be surprising." Uncomfortable with the way he was looking at her, she turned away from him and walked out of the kitchen. "I have to go to the office. I've got clients coming."

"Just so you know," her father called after her, "I'm letting him shower here."

"Whatever, Dad. As long as he's not here when I'm here."

"And he can do his laundry."

Unwilling to concede the last word, she shouted, "There better be hot water left for me at the end of the day!"

The situation was completely absurd. And to think she'd been certain that divorcing Greg would calm the wild roller coaster life she'd been living. Lauren just shook her head. Well, she was divorced all right. But now she had her father under her roof as well as under her skin, and her ex was still in her hair, too close for comfort.

Those two men seemed bent on keeping her frazzled.

She closed the front door and reached to smooth her hair. The scent of citrus wafted from her fingertips, forcing a frustrated sigh to issue from between her lips.

They were keeping her so frazzled that she couldn't remember something as simple as an orange.

Chapter Seven

Sex is like air, it's not important
unless you're not getting any.
~Unknown

Lauren's arms ached. She stepped back and lowered them to her sides, stretching her neck muscles to the left and then to the right. This kind of strenuous labor wasn't something she was used to. Her job entailed the flexing of her brain, not her biceps, triceps and deltoids.

She hadn't intended to get this involved in the project. In fact, after hiring Greg to do the dirty work two weeks ago, she'd intended to stay away from the barn altogether. But every evening after she locked the office doors, something pulled at her and she found herself driving to the swampy side of town.

Massaging one biceps and shoulder, then the other, she wrinkled her nose at the oily odor of metal polish that seemed to permeate her fingers and palms. This contraption had more brass on it than she'd realized.

After a couple of days standing around watching Greg work, she'd had to laugh when he'd pointed out her idleness.

"The job would go quicker," he'd told her, "if you picked up a cloth and started scrubbing."

Because she hadn't clarified her plans to sell off the animals piecemeal, Greg was cleaning the entire carnival ride—the roof, the animals, the platform. The whole shebang. She hadn't said a word to stop him.

When he'd suggested she shine up the brass railings and posts, she hadn't complained. The poles that secured the animals to the frame would go with each tiger, giraffe and horse she eventually sold, so she wasn't wasting her time there. Then the idea had come to her that some salvaging company might be interested in purchasing the railings, and shiny brass might sell for a higher price than if it was dull with tarnish.

"You're making great progress," Greg said, entering the barn. The brown bag he carried made a crisp, crinkling sound as he switched it from one arm to the next. "Sorry I'm late. I stopped to buy some paint and brushes."

He set the supplies on the workbench and slipped out of his jacket. While working on the merry-go-round each evening, they moved Greg's space heater into the main area of the barn. The small heater was no match for the vast space, but it did a fine job of taking the chill out of the air. As long as they wore sweaters or flannel shirts, they were warm enough.

"What colors did you buy?" For some odd reason, the idea of holding a paint brush in her hand made her suddenly giddy.

"Just red. For the roof," he told her.

Disappointment must have registered on her face because he quickly added, "I have to start at the top and work my way down."

Lauren nodded. "Of course." What she'd love, though, was to see one of those prancing Arabian horses come to life with a bright, fresh coat of glossy paint. The animals actually didn't look bad at all, now that all those years of dust and grime had been washed away.

He reached into the bag and pulled out several rolls of tape, two one-gallon buckets of paint and a packet of brushes. Then he handed her the receipt which she promptly stuffed into the rear pocket of her jeans without looking at it.

"Quit eyeing those animals," he told her. "I won't be painting those."

"What do you mean? Why not?"

One corner of Greg's mouth turned up. "You wouldn't let me paint your car with a brush, would you? I can paint a house. I can paint a fence or a piece of furniture. But I can't paint those." He indicated the merry-go-round menagerie with a small jerk of his head. "They need an airbrush and a talented hand."

Automatically, her gaze lowered to his hands, and she went still. It seemed that every molecule of air in the barn disappeared. Heat spread through her body as she remembered a time when he'd touched her with those talented hands, had slid them over her body until she'd... Her breath caught and held, and she battled the sudden, steamy thought by inhaling slowly, deeply.

She hooked her thumbs into her back pockets. "Well—"

"Don't worry. I've got it covered. I know a guy."

"I'll bet you do," she said softly. Lauren doubted there was a single soul in Sterling he didn't know.

"Don't worry," he repeated, grinning. "He owes me."

Half the people in town owed Greg money. And a lot of them weren't able to afford, or had never intended, to pay up. That's why he'd lost the hardware store. That's why their marriage had crumbled. Well, that was one reason, anyway.

Greg sighed. "A favor, Lauren. He owes me a favor."

There had been a time when his bartering skills had impressed and fascinated her. He once installed a countertop at Rapunzel's, the local beauty salon, and in exchange for the job he'd brought home a year's supply of coupons for hair cuts and manicures for her. He'd once brought home a bicycle for their neighbor's son that he'd swapped for a small home repair. Several summers running, he'd traded his work for a season of grass cutting and landscaping services.

Those who participated in bartering had developed a complicated third and fourth party system where work or products or services might be provided to someone the supplier had never even met in order to pay back a debt owed to another. As long as everyone kept up their end of the deals, the system worked. But over the years she'd seen that Greg's soft-hearted nature all too often left him holding the short end of the bargaining stick. Lauren preferred a 'you bill me, I'll bill you' business system which ensured that everyone involved was fairly compensated—with cold, hard currency.

"Okay," she told him. "No insult intended, Greg."

"None taken." He stripped the cardboard protectors off the paint brushes. "He won't airbrush all those animals for free. The job's too big. But he'll give you a good discount, I'm sure."

She reached out and picked up a colorful piece of cardboard. "I wouldn't feel comfortable with you using one of your favors for this job. I don't mind paying full price. I've taken on some new clients. Business is pretty good."

He paused for the briefest second, the look in his dark eyes impenetrable. "I'd like to do this for you. If you'll let me, that is."

The very air took on a heaviness that couldn't be ignored, and Lauren realized this could be a pivotal moment. He was making a kind offer, and her acceptance or refusal would have a momentous affect on their relationship.

She'd been angry with Greg for a long time. Too long, her father believed. Although the motives behind the emotion were strong—the lies he'd held firm to until it was too late, the poor business decisions he'd made, the damage he'd done to their financial security—Lauren was slowly coming to understand that she was the only one suffering from all her snarling and teeth gnashing.

Her dad was right. She was going to have to let go of the anger and negativity. And a good first step in that direction would be to graciously accept Greg's offer.

Tossing the thick paper wrapper onto the workbench, she smiled. "Okay."

His expression remained serious as he murmured, "Thanks."

Two tiny words. That's all they were. One from her. One from him. Yet in that short exchange they had expressed more to each other than they had in over a year.

"I should get back to polishing," she said, breaking the silence that was quickly turning awkward. "I only stopped to give my arms a break."

"And that roof's not going to paint itself." The

cellophane wrapper on one roll of tape popped under the pressure of his thumb.

Lauren picked up the can of brass polish and the jersey rag she'd left on the wooden platform. Greg set up an aluminum step ladder just a few feet away from her. She tipped the can of polish over her rag just as he climbed the rungs. She gave his firm, jean-clad butt a darting glance and immediately felt a dollop of the thick polish hit the top of her canvas sneaker with a plop.

"Well, shoot," she muttered, bending to swipe at the mess.

"You say something?"

"No, it's nothing."

Surely her shoe was ruined. The polish left behind a greasy looking stain.

What was wrong with her?

Every night this week, she'd come to the barn to work. Even though she'd told herself she wouldn't. And every night this week, she'd noticed some physical attribute of Greg's—the curve of his jaw, his taut shoulders, his brawny arms, his muscular thighs, and, tonight, his firm rump. The man didn't have an ounce of fat on his body. Taking another covert glance, she saw that he'd balanced his weight on his right leg, his left work boot perched on the next higher rung. The stance forced his right thigh muscle to tense. Lauren took her bottom lip between her teeth.

She'd left here each evening all hot and bothered, and she'd spent hours trying to block out the nagging ache that he caused to pulse down low in her torso.

If Greg were the only man flipping her 'on' switch, she'd have been scared to death. But, thank God, he wasn't. It wasn't all that long ago that she'd nearly drowned in the deep sea of Scott Shaw's eyes and she remembered paying particular attention to the way his suit fit his body.

Every women's magazine in the country had run at least one story touting the fact that females reached the height of their sexual desire in their late thirties. And wasn't it just Lauren's luck to be hitting her peak only to find herself divorced and too distrusting of relationships at the moment to even think about dating?

"You okay down there?" Greg asked.

"Yes, mm-hmm. I'm good." She straightened, frowning at the mess she'd made with all the wiping and smearing. Rather than clean up her shoe, all she'd done was spread the stain even more.

He was peering down at her. She told him, "I had a little mishap, is all."

He grinned, and she felt a small prickling sensation near her diaphragm. The lips he was using to smile at her had at one time driven her out of her mind with pleasure.

She directed her glassy-eyed gaze at a section of dulled brass railing and scrubbed at it with the cloth. "I've tried to get Dad involved in the renovations," she said, desperate to get the lustful images out of her head, "but I can't get him interested in anything but that computer."

Greg laughed. "Oh, he's interested in something else, I think."

"Yeah." She nodded as she rubbed the metal, the tarnish turning the white jersey black. "Surfing the net for names of medical conditions to fit symptoms he thinks he has." She turned the rag over and buffed the railing until it glistened.

"There might be a reason for that."

"Oh, yeah," she repeated. "He's stubbornly trying to prove that Doc Amos doesn't know what he's talking about."

Greg said no more, so she expounded. "Dad told me the other day that he was sure he had diabetes because his feet were tingling."

Having finished taping off a section of the roof facing, Greg climbed down off the ladder.

"I remembered that he'd asked me to buy him new laces for his shoes." She leaned on the railing. "I went into his closet and saw that his shoes were laced so tight they were cutting the circulation off in his feet."

She looked at him, expecting him to comment. But he only stood next to the ladder, his gaze steady on hers.

Finally, he gave her a small smile, and her traitorous heart thunked.

"It's a good thing you thought to check his shoes. I don't like the idea of Lew in pain."

He was a handsome man. There was no getting around it. She'd fallen in love with those dark good looks, hadn't she? But after all she'd been through over the past eighteen months or so, she'd thought she was over being affected by his smile, his eyes and the warmth in his voice.

"He's a royal pain." The instant the quip left her mouth, she regretted it. She sounded petty and mean, and she fought the urge to squirm under Greg's silent disapproval.

"I'm sorry. I shouldn't have said that. It's just... " She lifted her shoulders. "He complains so much.

When he's healthy as a horse. It doesn't make sense." She shrugged again. "And besides that, it's not easy getting used to having someone in the house again."

Her excuses sounded lame. Greg knew her father, knew full well that even on a good day he tended to be one big ball of pessimism. Yet Greg had never in his life said a negative word about the man.

She sighed. "I'll be nice. I promise."

Greg's smile shifted her heart into high gear, and she was actually relieved when he turned away from her and headed toward the work bench. Of course, that put his tight bottom into full view.

"When I said Lew was interested in something," he said, "I meant someone."

"What?" The idea was so ludicrous she laughed, but the gleam in Greg's jet black eyes when he glanced over his shoulder at her quickly snuffed out her amusement. "Who?"

"Norma Jean."

She moved to the workbench next to him. "You're joking, right?"

He chuckled and shook his head. Picking up the silver can opener, he began prying open one of the paint cans. "He's been talking about her an awful lot."

"What does that mean exactly, 'an awful lot'?"

The metal lid clattered against the workbench when Greg dropped it. "Two or three times over the past week he's brought up her name." He picked up a wooden paint stick and slapped it against his palm. "I've known Lew for a lot of years and this is the first time he's ever mentioned a woman."

"Well, naturally he'd talk about her. She made dinner for us a few nights. She even stopped by to eat with us once." Lauren shook out her polishing cloth and set it next to the paint can. "But she did it for me. She knows I've been stressed." She frowned. "I hope Dad doesn't make more out of this than there is. I don't want him to get his feelings hurt." She went quiet a moment, then tilted her head. "You really think he could be interested in her?"

"He's not dead, Lauren."

It seemed an impossible notion to imagine. Her dad and Norma Jean. Her dad and anyone.

"Maybe I should talk to him." She couldn't imagine starting a discussion with her father where the topic was his love life, so she quickly amended, "Maybe the one I should talk to is Norma."

Greg left the stick in the paint and started rolling up his sleeves. "Maybe you should let things be. Let them work it out."

She watched the way muscle and sinew played beneath the skin of his forearms as she murmured, "Yeah, you're probably right."

Why was it so easy to imagine his hands and lips on her? He used to do this amazing thing where he ran his fingers lightly along the indentation of her spine all the way up to her neck. Then he'd slowly make his way back down…

Hormones zipped through her like mini rockets and her mouth went dry.

"Listen, Greg—" she took a backward step to put some distance between them "—I think I'm going to take off. I'm… I'm kind of tired."

She wondered if the words sounded as breathy to him as they did to her.

"I'm only going to work for an hour or so," he said, clearly oblivious. "Then I'll be hitting the hay."

Visions of rolling around naked with him in a pile of sweet-smelling hay had her tossing her polishing rag onto the work bench and reaching for her purse and keys. "I'll see you later."

"Don't tell Lew I told you he talked about Norma Jean," he called after her. "He probably wouldn't like it."

"My lips are sealed."

As she drove toward town, she did her best to focus only on what Greg had suggested about her dad. He was seventy years old. Could he really be thinking of hooking up with Norma Jean?

There was no way possible that the feisty Norma would be attracted to her father. Of course, Norma saw him exactly for what he was—a sedentary and boring oldster. Lauren loved her dad and didn't want to see him hurt. She really should try to find some way to talk to him about this.

Try as she might, she couldn't ignore the dull achiness that pulsed in the deepest, most womanly part of her, and a powerful mental image of Greg's hands on her bare flesh assaulted her. She pressed her palm to her hot cheek. She could almost feel his touch, smell his skin, taste his kiss. "Stop," she whispered aloud and leaned forward to study the road.

She snapped on the air conditioner full blast and pointed the vents directly at her face and chest.

She couldn't even contemplate approaching her father or Norma about what might or might not be happening between them. How could she when her own wayward desires were so out of control?

* * *

"If you'll sign these letters, I'll mail them off today." Norma bustled into Lauren's office with several letters in her hand. "The Shaws certainly didn't look happy."

She lined up three documents in front of Lauren and held out an ink pen.

The office had been hopping for the past few days, the increased clientele they'd taken on forcing them to increase their office hours. Lauren didn't mind. The longer work days meant business was good. Better than good, actually. It also meant she was too tired to drive out to the barn to work on the merry-go-round with Greg in the evenings.

She took the pen from Norma and endorsed the letters. "They weren't. Mr. Shaw's upset with his son because he hasn't found a job. He was ragging on Scott, Jr pretty hard. Kept talking to him like he was twelve years old." Lauren shook her head. "Sure, he needs to earn some money, but... geez. I felt so bad for the kid that I finally offered him a job working out at the barn."

Norma scooped up the documents and tapped them smartly on the desktop. "I thought you hired Greg for that job?"

"I did," Lauren said, straightening the small pile of correspondence in her in box so she wouldn't have to make eye contact.

"It's not working out?"

"Oh, no," she told Norma. "It's working out fine. Greg's making good progress."

She'd rather die than admit she didn't trust herself to be alone with her ex husband for fear she might jump his bones.

"But there's plenty of work out there," she said, and hoped that would be sufficient explanation. She chuckled then. "Scott accepted my offer but then told me he couldn't start until next week because he had a paper due on Monday. I thought his father was going to pop a cork."

Norma rolled her eyes and shook her head. "I swear, teens are God's punishment for enjoying sex. I was so glad when mine finally grew all the way up."

Lauren wouldn't know a thing about raising children. She'd spent her late teens earning her undergrad degree, a good portion of her twenties going to law school, and her thirties had been focused on building her reputation and her business. She and Greg had talked about kids once or twice, but that perfect 'some day' had never seemed to arrive.

Seeing the way their marriage had fallen apart, she couldn't help but feel relieved there had been no children's lives to be ruined by their mistakes.

"I happened to overhear Mr. Shaw ask you out for dinner tonight."

Lauren nodded.

"I also heard you turn him down." Norma Jean's mouth flattened with disapproval.

She lifted a shoulder. "I don't like the idea of dating one of my clients."

"He's not a client," Norma pointed out.

"Not technically maybe, but... it's just... well..."

Norma Jean narrowed her eyes and waved the letters at her. "Okay, there's more to this story. I can tell. What gives?"

Lauren sighed, long and loud. "I don't know. I feel... I've been very... antsy lately."

"Antsy?"

She got up from her desk and paced to the window. There were several cars parked in the back lot.

"Something's off, Norma," she confessed.

"Something's going on. With my body. And my mind. I go out to the barn to work, and I can't pay attention to what I'm doing because I keep noticing the way Greg's jeans hug his thighs. And I missed some of the conversation with Scott Shaw because I was mesmerized by the way the man's mouth was forming words. All I kept thinking was how it would feel if—" She cut the thought off at the quick. Norma didn't need to be subjected to her naughty imaginings.

Her friend chuckled. "Lauren, honey, I know exactly what you're problem is. You need to have an orgasm."

"Norma!" she said, laughter and shock both pulling at her mouth.

Without missing a beat, Norma continued, "And not solo, Lauren. You need a man."

Sudden panic squashed Lauren's humor when she realized she was hearing the very words she'd been refusing to admit to herself. "I can't do that."

Norma Jean grinned. "It's like riding a bike, honey. Once you get on, it'll all come back to you."

Moving back to her desk, she said, "I don't mean I can't. I mean I... can't. I don't, you know... I don't have access to an available man."

Lauren could see Norma's eyes glittering. The woman was doing her best not to laugh.

"Well, you'd better find one," Norma said softly. "Your body's telling you what it needs. You need to listen."

She nipped her bottom lip. "Greg is completely off limits. And I can't... I can't—" she shook her head "—not with Scott Shaw. What if I went out with him and we ended up in bed? Which, knowing how I'm feeling, is exactly what would happen. Maybe. Probably." She grimaced. "If things don't go well for his son in court, I'd be mortified."

"Lauren, Mr. Shaw seems like a rational man," Norma said. "He's not going to blame you if his son has to pay a fine, sexy romp or no sexy romp. I just read an article in Cosmo that said, in some circumstances, it's okay to mix business with pleasure." Norma winked at her. "You'll work something out, I'm sure."

Lauren squeezed her eyes closed and scrubbed at her temples. It had been so long since she'd had sex, she couldn't imagine getting naked with any man. No, that wasn't true. The heady state of her libido made it easy to imagine, but the idea of actually having sex with a virtual stranger seemed like behavior that was far too reckless. At least, for anyone with good sense.

"Speaking of sexy men," Norma quipped. "I'm worried about your dad."

The whip-lash speed of the subject change made Lauren's eyes go wide. But before she could respond, Norma Jean said, "I think Lew's coming down with something."

"You talked to him?" She'd been so busy the past few evenings with research and argument writing for one of her new cases that she hadn't arrived home until her father had gone to bed, and he'd been tucked behind the morning paper when she left the house this morning.

Norma nodded. "I think he may have strep or something. His tongue looks red and irritated."

"He didn't say anything this morning." Realizing what Norma said, she asked, "You saw his tongue?"

"He didn't sound good when we chatted on the phone this morning, so I offered to bring him a cup of chicken soup from the deli for lunch today."

Lauren absently centered the buckle of her belt. "I'm sorry. You shouldn't have to listen to his complaints, and you didn't have to drive all the way out there. You should have transferred his call to me. I could have taken him some soup."

"I was happy to have lunch with him." She smiled sheepishly and admitted, "He didn't call the office, Lauren. I called him."

"Oh. Well, then. But..." Lauren went quiet for a split second. "Why would you do that?"

Excitement brightened Norma's expression. "Because I like him, silly. Lew's a great guy. I had a wonderful time when we had dinner at your house. I've called a couple of times just to say hi. I can't believe I hadn't thought of him as possible date material before now. I asked him out to dinner but he turned me down." She grinned. "But I'm not giving up. A no on the first request is fairly normal. Men from my generation aren't used to women doing the asking."

Lauren just stood there staring. She really couldn't believe what she was hearing.

Norma's smile wilted a tad. "It's okay, isn't it? If I have dinner with your Dad?"

"W-well," she stammered. She couldn't get over her shock. "Sure... but—" she swept her fingers across her bangs, fighting through her confusion for the right words to express her feelings "—the two of you are so... different."

Norma Jean's grin was back, full throttle. "Diversity is the spice of life, sweetie."

She still didn't get it. "But all Dad does is sit in the house all day. He goes to get his hair cut and pick up his prescriptions once a month. He's like a hibernating bear. You, you're a racecar driver on the speedway of life."

Cutting a wide arc through the air with the letters in her hand, Norma waved off Lauren's concern. "Oh, now. We're not all that different. Lew's a lot like that old carrousel you've been working on. He just needs a little dusting off, a little oiling up and to have his on button pushed, is all." Her brown eyes shined. "If anyone can turn him on, Lauren, it's me."

Lauren didn't know whether to chuckle or cover her ears.

"Anyway," Norma said, her tone sobering, "Lew thinks he's got an infection in his salivary glands. He gave me some long name for it."

Apparently her father had been surfing the medical websites again.

Norma slipped the ink pen behind her ear. "I suggested he go see his doctor, but he said he didn't have one."

"He has one. He's just not speaking to Doc Amos at the moment."

"Charlie Amos? I know him."

"Dad and Doc have known each other for ages," Lauren said. "Dad's just got his knickers in a twist, is all. I was hoping he'd get over it by now. I'd love it if Dad felt he had a doctor he could consult when he needed to."

"Charlie's wife, Katie, is a good friend of mine." Norma Jean tapped her chin with the letters. "Maybe I can work on that situation for you." Then she pulled the pen from behind her ear and headed for the door. "I'm getting on these letters before it gets too much later."

"Norma," Lauren said, making the woman turn around in the doorway. "I noticed that Dad filled the candy dish in the living room with lemon drops. I'll bet his mouth is sore because he's overdosing on them." When Norma looked at her dubiously, she shrugged. "It's happened in the past."

"Ah. Okay." Norma smiled. "I hope his problem really is that simple."

"I'm sure it is. I'll talk to him when I get home."

Lauren sat down at her desk and reached for one of the envelopes sitting in her 'in' box. Well, how about that? Norma Jean had asked her dad out on a date.

But he had turned down the offer. Why on earth would he do a thing like that?

Had Norma Jean really called him sexy?

She slid her letter opener beneath the envelope's flap, those other words of advice Norma had spoken coming back to haunt her.

You need to have an orgasm.

It was the truth. Lauren couldn't deny it.

She liked sex as much as the next woman. Memories of the delicious times she'd spent with Greg in their king-sized bed made her mouth stretch into a grin. She dropped the silver letter opener into the drawer and fanned herself with the envelope.

Now wasn't that just her luck? Hormones on a rampage, and here she sat with no husband, no boyfriend, no man at all. What in the world would Cosmo have to say about that?

Chapter Eight

Slowly wheels go round and round,
and cogs begin to grind and pound.
~Oompa Loopa

Lauren snapped her cell phone shut and tossed it onto the passenger seat next to her purse. Greg had used the code words. Words she hadn't heard since the two of them had split. The phrase that, while they had been married, had never failed to make her grin and set her anticipation spinning like a turbine.

I've got something to show you.

Of course, he had no idea he was speaking in code. He never had. But that's what had always made it so much fun. He'd plot and plan and organize surprises for her only to tip her off by using the same habitual expression to get her to a specific place at a specific time.

I've got something to show you.

Years ago, he'd called her out of the blue. Norma Jean had interrupted her while she'd been with a client, requesting that she take Greg's 'important' phone call. Lauren remembered how annoyed she'd been when he'd asked her to meet him in a park on the outskirts of Sterling. The office hadn't been open long, and she'd been struggling for a foothold in Sterling's legal door. She was in the middle of a meeting, she'd told him in a huff. She had a business she was trying to kick start. She couldn't just up and leave her office in the middle of a work day. But then he'd said those magic words.

I've got something to show you.

Her sudden flash of irritation had been no match for the warmth that had spread through her at the sound of his silky voice. After only a moment's hesitation, she'd asked Norma to reschedule her afternoon appointments and wrapped up her meeting as quickly as she could before setting off on what she knew would be an adventure. And she'd been so glad she had!

Greg had hired a hot air balloon, and they'd shared a romantic champagne lunch while sailing across the county among the scudding clouds.

The memory made her smile even now as she drove out of town and headed toward Skeeter Neck Road. Opening her window, she let the balmy Indian summer breeze blow into the car. It was a glorious day for late October.

Lauren had decided to stay away from Greg, and she'd been successful in doing just that for a week and a half. She'd been leaving early enough that they hadn't crossed paths at her house, either.

However, her 'Big O' problem, as Norma Jean had shrewdly coined it, continued to rage. The office had become a revolving door of new clients, so she hadn't even had time to think about an 'O', large, small or in between. Well, that wasn't entirely true. When a woman had an 'O' needing release—and in her case it really was a Big O—it had a way of creeping into her thoughts whether she wanted it to or not. So although she had thought about it, she hadn't dwelled on it.

Much.

Lauren focused on Greg's phone call and those magic words he'd uttered. She hoped his surprise was at least one air-brushed carousel animal. More than one would be extra special.

In her mind's eye, she pictured one of those magnificent Arabians painted a glistening snow-white, the feather plumes of its headdress a rich shade of blue or fuchsia or some other bold color. She could almost imagine herself riding one of those beauties, round and round, to the tinny but gay sound of pipe organ music. How fun!

She sat a little straighter. What she should conjure were visions of raking in the dough when all the doting parents and grandparents, aunts and uncles started buying those carousel figures for the children in their lives. Having any one of those prancing horses for her very own would make any little girl feel like a fairy princess. And boys would have a blast on imaginary safaris with a lion or tiger or bear. Lauren made a mental note of that excellent marketing ploy.

The sky was nearly dark when she arrived, the barn and surrounding property quiet and still. One of the doors was wide open and pale light spread across the grassy expanse.

She didn't see Greg at first, and ended up calling his name.

"Hey, there," he called, appearing in the

doorway that led to the back room, a terry towel in his hands.

When she saw him, she smiled. It actually felt good to see him and not get all mired in anger. "Got here as soon as I could. I've been really busy at work." She shrugged out of her jacket and tossed it on a sawhorse.

"Yeah, Lew told me you've been at the office a lot."

She looked at the neatly stacked lumber sitting in the corner, an addition since her last visit. "A job?"

He nodded. "I'm doing some work for Jo Leigh Stapleton. Put in a few cabinets for her today."

The familiar name caught Lauren's attention. "I didn't know she was still in town. She was in my graduating class." Jo Leigh's last name had been Ewing back then. Just a year after high school graduation, Lauren attended Jo Leigh's and Jim Stapleton's wedding. Over the years, though, she and Jo Leigh had lost touch.

"She told me you and she went to school together." He hung the towel on the metal door latch. "She lives over in Maplewood."

The older neighborhood was located just outside of Sterling. Maplewood had grown until

it was now nearly a town of its own with several shopping centers and gas stations and a post office.

"Shame about her husband," Greg said.

"What happened to Jim?"

"He was firefighter. Died when a house collapsed during a fire a couple years ago."

"Oh, Greg, that's terrible." How could she have missed reading about that in the newspapers? Or hearing about it from friends? "Did they have kids?"

Greg nodded. "A little girl. She's around ten or so. Cute kid. Looks just like Jo Leigh. You want a beer or a soda or something?"

"No, thanks. I'm can't stay long."

Again, Greg nodded; then he looked over at the merry-go-round. "I finished the roof. Would have done a little more, but... well, I've been busy, myself."

"That's okay," she told him. "You have to take care of paid jobs first. Hey, how is Scott working out? Is he a help, or a hindrance?"

Greg smiled. "He's a help. Doesn't always show up when he's supposed to, but he seems like a good kid."

"She looks great." Lauren had no idea why she thought of the merry-go-round as having a gender.

She felt a little self-conscious, but quickly discovered there was no need for it.

"She does, doesn't she?" Greg turned to follow her gaze.

The fresh coat of glossy red paint gleamed even in the dim light thrown by the barn's single, bare bulb hanging overhead from the rafters. Gold trim set off the roof to perfection. Sharp lines and edges, no drips; he'd done a professional job. But she didn't see that any of the animals sported new paint.

She was curious to know what he wanted to show her, but before she could ask, he glanced her way, his handsome face expressing that he had something on his mind.

"You seen your dad lately?"

She lifted one shoulder. "Like he told you, the office has kept me hopping."

Greg meandered toward the merry-go-round. "I think he might be missing you."

"Come on. Don't lecture me about my dad. I have to work when the clients are there. He understands that. There will be times when business is slow and I can be around more." She wouldn't have to work so hard if Greg hadn't nearly ruined her financially, but she didn't bother mentioning it. "He's got you stopping in every morning. And Norma Jean's been calling him several times a week."

"Norma Jean." Greg gave a half grin. "She asked Lew to go out to dinner with her, did you know that?"

"She's asked more than once," she said with a nod. "And Dad keeps turning her down. I guess I should talk to him about that." She paused a moment. "If I can figure out how to tell him that having a little fun won't kill him without getting my head bitten off, that is."

Greg chuckled. "I think she surprised him. At least, that's how it seemed to me when he talked about it." He slid his hands into his back pockets. "As if he'd been sucker thumped with a feather pillow." When he got close enough, he reached up and grasped the brass railing. "Want me to talk to him about it? You know, guy to guy?"

She hesitated a mere second before saying, "I'll do it. He's not your problem anymore."

He looked at her a moment, his dark gaze going flat. "He might not be my father-in-law, Lauren, but he's still my friend."

Dipping her chin, she noticed a smudge of dirt on her leather pump. "I know you care about him,

Greg. I didn't mean to insinuate otherwise. I just meant that, well, as his daughter, I should be the one to, um—" she offered him an apologetic smile "—take on the dangerous jobs. You know as well as I do that Dad doesn't like to be told what to do."

The tension left his shoulders. "That's an understatement. All right, then. You take him on. But if you need back up, I'm your man."

Their eyes met and held.

No man had the right to look that good in a plain gray t-shirt and blue jeans.

Needing somewhere else to focus her gaze, Lauren glanced down the front of her and swiped at imaginary lint on the thighs of her black wool trousers.

"So," she hedged lightly, "you called me out here to show me something."

"Yeah. Yeah, I did."

His smiled again and his eyes shined like polished onyx. She'd seen that look a thousand times while they had been married.

She once went away for a weekend to attend a seminar, and when she returned, he'd built a shed in the back yard. She'd only remembered complaining once about the garage clutter, but when she drove into the driveway, he was there to open the garage door and wave at her to drive inside the tidy space.

Then there had been their first Christmas together. He had spent an entire day hanging strands of lights from the house. The winter sky had been dark by the time she'd arrived home from the office, and she'd been absolutely delighted when she'd turned the corner and seen their home lit up like a colorful gingerbread house.

The man positively loved to give surprises.

"Come on. I want you to do the honors." He reached out his hand to her.

Lauren didn't hesitate. "The honors?" she asked, hurrying to him and sliding her palm into his. His calloused fingertips were warm as they closed over hers, their rough texture triggering memories of when he'd touched other, more sensitive parts of her body. He pulled her up onto the merry-go-round's platform.

"I oiled the mechanics of this thing," he told her, zigzagging through the animals on his way toward the center core, pulling her along behind him.

He let go of her hand finally and reached to open a panel door, then stepped back. The opening was filled with knobs and levers, bolts and cogs.

"That one." He pointed to the biggest lever. "Got to be the main switch, don't you think?"

It was so silly, but Lauren had the funniest feeling in the pit of her stomach; she was both excited and nervous, and she had the craziest urge to laugh.

She looked from the lever to him. "You really think it will work?"

He tossed up his hands before resting them on his thighs. "As old as this thing is, it may not. But we won't find out until you give it a try."

The smile on her face couldn't have been bigger as she reached for the rubber handle. It took two hefty tugs to loosen the lever and lift it into the on position.

No music played and no lights flashed, but ever so slowly, the platform began to move. The wood creaked and thumped as the carousel came to life.

Lauren let out a tiny shout, pinched the fabric of Greg's t-shirt and gave a quick tug, urging him to move. "Come on! Come on!" She jumped onto the platform, her heart thundering, and she laughed when she saw he'd followed her lead. She felt like a kid at her first carnival.

The inner-most circle of Arabians danced slowly, up and down. She and Greg fell into the fancy sleigh located in the center ring. Next to them a circus zebra undulated, its motion reminiscent of a gallop.

Gazing from one animal to another, she sat there shaking her head in complete and utter wonder.

"Oh, Greg," she whispered on an exhalation. "Can you believe it? It works. It really works."

She shifted on the seat and looked at him, knowing full well that the delight thrumming through her shined in her eyes.

A champagne lunch in a hot air balloon.

A new shed and a clutter-free garage.

A thousand multi-colored lights to brighten her Christmas.

And now a merry-go-round overflowing with prancing animals.

This man was filled with surprises, some practical, others utterly thrilling.

Lauren reached up and placed the flat of her hand on his chest. Later, when she had time to analyze the moment closer, she would realize that touching him was her first and fatal blunder, but right now she was too caught up in the enchanting surprise he'd given her.

The kiss started so astonishingly quickly that she hadn't time to think, let alone notice which of them had initiated it. His mouth was lusciously hot and moist, heavenly against her lips. She parted for him, and immediately tasted a faint peppermint sweetness on his tongue.

Greg had always been the best kisser.

The old wood slats scraped the dirt floor in places and the cogs beneath the platform ticked as Lauren shifted yet again, parting her knees until she was straddling Greg's lap. She felt the heat of him seep through the fabric of her trousers when he cradled her bottom in his palms. The merry-go-round spun, but the resulting breeze did nothing to cool the fire flaming inside her.

She pressed herself against the hardness of him, and the soft groan that issued from deep in her throat harmonized with the grinding of the metal mechanics. Their kiss turned wild, almost frantic. She slid her fingers up his shoulders and neck, delving them into his thick, black hair. He kneaded her thighs with his strong hands and then slid them down to massage her butt, pulling her more tightly against him.

The need to feel his skin against hers became overwhelming. She drew away from him and tugged at his t-shirt. Gathering the fabric in trembling fingers, she was relieved when he helped her pull it off his body.

His hands were on her, everywhere it seemed; her thighs, her waist, her arms, her breasts. She'd only succeeded in unfastening three of the buttons on her blouse when they were kissing again; hard, hungry kisses that made her feel weak and trembling and needy.

"Lauren," he whispered against her mouth.

Don't talk. Don't talk! She wanted to shout, but couldn't seem to find her voice.

She kissed him again to silence him, slid her fingers up his neck, over his jaw, but on the outskirts of her brain something felt... off. Odd. Out of sync.

Lauren tried to ignore the feeling, closing her eyes tight, shifting her weight forward, running a palm across the back of his neck. However, the peculiarity—whatever it was—only became more pronounced, refusing to be discounted.

Lifting her chin, she gazed through the strands of hair that had fallen across her face. Evidently, Greg thought she was offering him her neck, and he nuzzled the sensitive skin with his lips and tiny nips of his teeth. Heat shot through her, liquid electricity flowing through her torso and limbs.

Inhaling a ragged breath, she reached up and pushed the hair out of her eyes. When he dipped his tongue into the hollow of her neck, she sighed and nearly forgot all about the weird sense that something was wrong. All she wanted to do was surrender to the hot pulse that beat deep in the center of her being.

But then she saw it, and her eyes went wide. She sat back, her gaze darting from the prancing animals to the workbench on the far side of the barn as they passed by it.

The merry-go-round was traveling in reverse. The horses, tigers, bears, zebras were all circling tail-end first as if competing in some bizarre, backward race.

Lauren felt a cool breeze on her bare chest and realized that Greg had finished unbuttoning her blouse, evidently oblivious to the fact that she'd stopped participating in the foreplay.

Just as his hands glided over her lace-covered breasts, she said, "Stop." Her voice was dry and hoarse and had come out as a mere whisper, so she repeated the order.

He let go of her, his gaze darting to her face.

"What is it?" he said, his tone husky with desire. "What's wrong?"

It was as if the clicking and grinding cogs snickered at her; jeering in some secret circus cipher. Then she realized why she felt that way. The reverse motion of the merry-go-round was a huge, ironic metaphor for what this single, rash deed would do to her life.

Is this what she wanted? To make love to her ex-husband?

Although this episode of luscious horniness most probably would assuage her need—solve her Big O problem—what would it do to her and Greg's relationship?

Would he expect them to get back together?

Would she expect them to get back together?

Her eyes went wide and she planted the flat of her hand on his chest.

"I won't go backward." She pushed herself off his lap and staggered a step or two before regaining her balance on the moving platform. Her blouse hung open and her face flamed as she fully grasped the enormous gaffe she'd nearly made.

"What?" Greg scooted straighter on the seat, combing the fingers of both hands through his tangled hair.

He looked as if he were awakening from a haze.

Guilt pinged her like a storm of freezing hail, but it was much too late to do anything about that now.

Lauren sidestepped the zebra, her arm brushing against the peeling black paint on its nose, and she stepped off the revolving carousel. She hurried toward the sawhorse where she'd left her purse and keys.

"Lauren!"

Greg must have turned off the conveyor because the rhythm of the groaning and ticking slowed. Only after shoving her arms into her jacket did she begin to fasten the buttons on her blouse. She was still working the buttons when she turned to face him.

She had no idea what to say to him, how to explain her crazy behavior.

He was sliding his arms and head into his t-shirt as he stalked toward her.

"You're fired," she told him, bluntly. She buttoned her blouse all wrong and the hem hung cock-eyed. "I want you out of the barn, Greg."

Out of my life, she wanted to add, but didn't. There was no sense in hurting his feelings. She just wanted him away from her. Someplace where she didn't have to see him. Didn't have to be affected by him.

"I know I told you that you could stay. But I've changed my mind. You've got to go." With that, she snagged the strap of her purse and turned toward the door.

"Lauren, wait. Can't we talk about this?"

He caught up with her and reached out for her forearm.

"Why are you angry with me?" Confusion knit his brow. "I, uh, I only did what I... " His tone lowered as he gently finished, "What I thought you wanted."

God, how she had wanted it! She'd nearly climaxed while straddling his lap and she'd still been fully dressed.

Her skin burned, but it wasn't with need—it was with embarrassment.

"I'm not angry with you, Greg." She pulled her arm out of his grip and headed for the door. "I'm angry with me."

Chapter Nine

Given the choice between two evils,
I always choose the one I've never tried before.
~Mae West

"I'm sorry, Ms. Woods. I can't help you."
Lauren folded her hands on her desk, silently guessing she wasn't the first lawyer in town to refuse to help this young woman.

"But you have to. If I'm convicted of a crime, I'll lose my scholarship."

Glancing at the forms in front of her, Lauren said, "I've read the police report. You don't have a leg to stand on."

Diana Woods self-consciously shifted her casted

foot a couple of inches to the right, and Lauren instantly regretted her choice of words.

Her mouth turned down apologetically. "Let me rephrase, Ms. Woods. You can't fight this and win when you were caught red-handed."

"But I wasn't. I didn't have anything on me when the police caught me." The declaration was made with a good amount of smug pride. Then she muttered, "I'd have gotten away if I hadn't tripped down those stairs and broken my damn ankle."

The report filed by police stated that Diana possessed no stolen goods when they apprehended her. But there had been enough evidence for an arrest, and the precise phrase to describe her capture would not have been 'red-handed' but 'red-butted.'

Diana Woods had filched the T-bone from the Stop 'N Shop's meat department by tucking the steak beneath her jacket and into the back waistband of her pants. It had been her bad luck to slam into the chest of the strip mall's security guard on her way out of the store. The guard had become instantly suspicious of her guilty countenance and had detained her. When the shop's owner appeared and an accusation had been made, Diana had fled the scene. She'd ditched the meat somewhere along her escape route, but the evidence had been clear.

"You had blood all over the backside of your jeans," Lauren pointed out.

The nineteen-year-old didn't flinch. "You could argue that it was my time of the month."

"Were you standing on your head at some point that day?" Lauren leaned back in her chair and crossed her arms. "Or do you have some deformity that causes you to menstruate from the small of your back?"

Diana's blue eyes narrowed slightly, and Lauren could tell she was seriously debating her answer.

"Before you speak," Lauren cautioned, "you should seriously consider the consequences of going into a court and lying to a judge."

The young woman's cast scraped against the hardwood floor. "But I won't be lying."

"Ah, I see." Lauren nodded. "You want me to lie for you."

Over the course of her career, this wasn't the first time the suggestion had been made to Lauren that she go into court and lie to a judge. Expressing the request in a blunt, no-nonsense fashion, as she'd just done for Diana, was usually enough to have these people feeling contrite and backing down. But the tactic wasn't working today.

"That's exactly what I want," Diana said, looking somewhat relieved. "The other lawyers I've talked to haven't seemed to understand that."

Lauren's smile contained very little humor. "Oh, I'm sure they understood perfectly." Then she repeated, "I'm sorry, Ms. Woods. I can't help you."

"But I'll lose my scholarship."

Lauren sighed. "We've been over all this." She stood, resting her fingertips on the top of the desk.

"Please, please, if you'll just listen to me. I need that scholarship," Diana stressed again. "It covers my tuition. The money I earn from my job barely pays the rent. I have very little money left over for food and utilities. I have eaten almost nothing but rice and noodles for three years. Do you have any idea what that's like? It was my birthday. I wanted a little protein. Is that so evil?"

Evil, no. Illegal, yes. But Lauren remained silent.

Diana Woods frowned, evidently upset that Lauren showed no pity. The young woman struggled out of the chair and reached for her crutches.

"I can see you're not going to help me," she told Lauren.

"If you're determined to lie about what happened, then you're right. I can't help you."

Diana hobbled to the door, the rubber tip of one crutch thumping into the jamb. "I'll find someone. I will. I need that scholarship."

Norma Jean's voice was cheery as she ushered the young woman out the front door.

Lauren went to the window overlooking the back parking lot.

"You okay?" Norma asked, and without waiting for a replay, she said, "I want to compliment you on your patience. That girl's a piece of work, isn't she? I can't believe she thought you would lie for her. To a judge, no less."

Norma had obviously been eavesdropping.

"She wasn't interested in a thing you had to say. If you ask me, Diana Woods is her own worst enemy."

Making her way back to her desk, Lauren nodded. "You can say that again."

* * *

"You are planning to restore those animals, right? And sell them off, one by one?" Scott Shaw, Sr. couldn't seem to take his eyes off the merry-go-round. "I don't know much about antiques, but we must be looking at a small fortune."

Now here was a man with some business sense. Hearing him voice the very same conclusion she'd come to did Lauren's heart good. "There's a guy coming next week to give me an estimate. Apparently, he's talented with an airbrush."

Scott climbed up onto the platform. "This thing's amazing. Where did it come from?"

"I don't really know."

His gaze darted from one animal to another, and she could tell from the look on his face that he was doing some earnest deliberating.

"You'll need a base of some kind," he told her.

Lauren hadn't thought of that.

"I'm not an engineer, but I'd think you'd need something substantial to keep everything upright and stable. Kids love to climb. A sturdy wooden box, maybe?" Scott's eyelids tensed slightly as he looked at her. "You know a good carpenter?"

The symmetry of his features—cheekbones, eyes and brows—made for a very attractive face. Lauren felt overheated and focused her gaze elsewhere.

During their previous meetings, he'd worn dark business suits. But this morning he'd shown up at the barn in khakis and a thick, cable knit sweater in a mottled brown that fit him well and looked great with his tawny hair.

"As a matter of fact, I do," she said.

He nodded, his attention once again on the carousel animals. "So we're, ah, doing some sanding today? Getting these babies ready for paint?"

"We?" She smiled. "I'm surprised to see you. I was expecting your son."

Scott stepped off the merry-go-round and walked toward her. "Oh, Scotty will be along shortly, I'm sure."

Lauren didn't have the heart to tell him that his son had only turned up for work a few times and he'd logged in less than eight hours total. At this rate, it would take the young man months to earn back the money his father had paid Lauren.

His woodsy cologne tinged the air when he came close. Scott reached out and took a lock of her hair between his fingers and thumb.

"He told me he was working for you today," he said softly. "And since I haven't been able to talk you into going out with me, I thought I'd come here. Spend some time with you. Offer up a little free labor so you can see what a great guy I am."

"I might have missed you. I'm not always here

when Scott comes. We've set up an honor system. He keeps a log of his hours in the notebook over on the workbench."

"I didn't know if you'd be here or not." His tone was silky soft as he lifted her hair first to his nose, then briefly to his cheek. "But whenever I take chances, lady luck often smiles on me."

His mouth pulled back into a small, sexy smile, and he let her hair flutter through his fingers.

"Lady luck, huh?" She parroted the phrase simply because she wasn't sure what else to say. His blatant flirting left her a little discombobulated.

"Yeah. I don't know if I've told you this but—" he inched a little closer "—I've wanted to kiss you since we first met."

He was near enough that she could see the steel-gray that flecked his blue irises, and his warm breath brushed her cheek.

Surrendering to temptation would be all too easy. All she had to do was lean toward him the slightest bit. Or reach out and finger the sleeve of his sweater. A simple smile would be all the signal necessary to let him know she was receptive.

Rather than doing any of these things, she chose instead to remind him, "Your son could walk through the door at any moment. You don't want him seeing us acting..." She paused, searching for just the right word. "Reckless."

The reality of the situation didn't sober him in the least.

"Scotty's a big boy. I'm sure he's seen worse."

Her mouth flattened quirkily as she did her best to suppress a grin. She shook her head.

Scott's tone softened to a whisper. "Lauren, I haven't been able to get you out of my mind."

The sincerity in his expression made her smile, but she still wasn't willing to let him take her to the place he wanted to go. She reached up and patted his cheek softly. "I have a solution for that."

His eyebrows lifted slightly, unconcealed curiosity—or was that desire—brightening his baby blues.

Lauren grinned as she lifted her hand and tilted her head. "Work."

He looked down at the fresh square of fine sandpaper she offered and he laughed.

They made small talk as they scraped and sanded a snarling lion, Lauren working on the head and mane, Scott focusing on the tail end. He questioned her about her divorce, and she commented on it vaguely, focusing on how the resulting financial situation forced her to move her father in with her for the time being. She learned Scott was an insurance broker and that he specialized in providing life and health insurance for the employees of large companies. Selling insurance wasn't his only responsibility. He also managed the group of people working at the brokerage firm who assisted with corporations' employee enrollment and helped to resolve benefit issues. He described himself as a people person who actually enjoyed the long hours he was required to work; he was a problem solver who found his job satisfying. It didn't hurt that the pay was excellent.

Lauren was learning that they had a lot in common.

"So what's it like?" he asked her. "Living with your dad again."

"It's not bad." She brushed fine grit sandpaper against the lion's nose. "I'm at the office or the courthouse a lot. So I don't see Dad all that much. At least, not through the work week, anyway. We're not stepping on each other's toes, if that's what you mean."

Scott blew across the lion's back and a small cloud of wood dust billowed. "When did your parents divorce? Where's your mom?"

Lauren stopped sanding.

"I'm sorry," he said. "I didn't mean to intrude."

"No, no. It's okay," she assured him softly. "My mom... died when I was a kid." The smile she flashed was small and tight and looked more like a grimace, she was sure. "Even after all these years it's still difficult to talk about. She had cancer. The doctors weren't sure where it started, but by the time they discovered it, it had metastasized to her bones." Lauren let her gaze trail to the far side of the barn. "She suffered a lot near the end. It was hard. For all of us."

She felt the penetrating warmth of him when he covered her hand with his. Their eyes met.

"I really am sorry." He gave her hand a squeeze before releasing it. "I didn't mean to bring up bad memories."

Lauren looked away. "It's okay." She liked the way he didn't hesitate to comfort her. A lot of men would have felt awkward with the discussion. Inhaling deeply, she went back to sanding.

"Your dad ever remarry?"

She shook her head. "He's never even dated."

Surprise flickered across his face. "That's a lot of years to be alone."

Lauren had tried to broach the subject of dating

Norma Jean with her father, but she hadn't completed the first sentence before he had twisted the 'relationship' conversation she'd planned into a knotted lecture about kicking Greg out of the barn. Scoldings were hard to swallow when you were thirty-eight. She'd let the matter drop, but she did plan to bring it up again when he was feeling less crotchety.

She glided her fingertips over the lion's smooth nose. "How about your parents?"

"They're snowbirds," Scott told her. "They spend summers in Maryland at their place on Deep Creek Lake, and they winter in the Keys. When Scotty was young, we used to fly down for a couple of long weekends in Florida every summer. Having the place to ourselves was great." He cocked his head. "I hadn't realized it until now, but we haven't been in several years." Then he frowned. "Speaking of my kid—" he glanced toward the door "—I wonder where he is."

Lauren stood, clapping the dust from her palms. "He's a teenager." She pulled her cell phone from her pocket and saw that she and Scott had been working and chatting for nearly forty minutes. "Probably got caught up with his friends."

Scott pressed his palm against the lion's

muscular hunch and pushed himself to a stand. "Well, if he told you he'd be here, he should be here. I'll speak to him about it."

She chuckled at his stern tone and he looked chagrinned.

"You think I'm too hard on him, don't you?" he asked.

Lauren shook her head and held up her hands. "I'm certainly not the person to tell you how to raise your kid."

"No, seriously. I'd like your opinion. Scotty doesn't see much of his mother, so I've been left on my own."

Teetering on a tight rope twenty feet in the air would be less dangerous than criticizing a man's parenting skills.

"As far as I can see, you're doing a good job," she told him. "Your son is as polite and respectful as any other college freshman I've met."

Scott captured her forearm and let his hand slide to her wrist. "And that was a nice, innocuous answer." He looked into her eyes. "Now tell me what you really think."

"Oh, come on." She rolled her eyes. But when she saw that he meant to get an answer out of her, she turned thoughtful. "Well, he does need to mature a little, I guess. Think before he acts. But that comes at different ages for different people. At least, it does from what I've seen. However, I think you could help him along if you would stop calling him Scotty. Makes him sound like a twelve-year-old."

He blinked several times, and his lips parted slightly. "Whoa," he breathed. "I never realized."

Sensing that the moment was about to turn unwieldy, Lauren grinned and tried spinning the conversation in a different direction. "Were you a responsible teen?"

Humor immediately shimmered in his gaze. "Are you kidding? I was ornery as they come."

Lauren stepped off the platform. "Somehow, I don't have a problem imagining that."

"I was the kind of kid who would break into a place like this." He looked from the door to the ceiling to the far side of the barn. "Not to do any vandalizing, of course. But I would have fiddled with this contraption until I got it working. And I'd have taken a free ride just for the bragging rights."

Her smile broadened. "If you need bragging rights, feel free to take a ride."

"It runs?"

"Well, yes... if you don't mind riding backward."

"Mind if I have a look?" He'd already turned away from her, making his way to the core of the carousel.

She heard the panel hinges squeak, and then metal clanked against metal as he fiddled with the levers and switches.

"Let's try this," he called.

Some of the lights flashed on and the tinny sounds of organ music floated on the air as the merry-go-round slowly began to turn.

Forward.

Lauren clapped her hands and laughed with pure delight, watching Scott jump onboard and wave as he passed her by. He climbed atop the lion they had just been sanding. She pressed her fingertips against her lips, unable to stop grinning behind them.

She had thought it best to avoid getting involved with Scott because she was his son's lawyer. But he was such a nice guy. Not to mention good looking. And they had much in common; they were both ambitious, hard-working and no-nonsense when it came to their careers.

Lauren lifted her hand in a reciprocal wave when he circled around again, a silly grin lighting his handsome face.

Maybe, just maybe, he was the man to get her life moving in the right direction.

Chapter Ten

Nobody tells me. Nobody keeps me informed.
I make it 17 days come Friday since
anybody spoke to me.
~Eeyore, from the Gloomy Place
in the Hundred Acre Wood

"I hope none of this stuff is spicy. My reflux will have me burping stomach acid all night long."

Lovely image to sit down to dinner with, Lauren thought as she watched her dad pick up his napkin and eye the take out containers dubiously.

"Stay away from the chicken with garlic sauce," she warned. "There's roast pork with snow peas, beef with broccoli and shrimp with cashews. I bought both steamed and fried rice. You should probably stick with the steamed." She picked up a pair of chopsticks. "Oh, and I ordered you a spring roll. I know how you love those."

He only grunted while he reached for the waxed paper bag housing the fried roll. "How about duck sauce?"

"Right here. I remembered to ask for extra." She handed him several packets.

Lauren used her chopsticks to serve herself a portion of fluffy, white rice and spicy chicken. She sighed. "This is nice, huh?"

"It's a real treat."

She glanced at her dad over the glistening morsel of chicken she balanced between her sticks unable to tell if he was being facetious. The chicken was tender, the slightly sweet sauce harmonizing perfectly with the bite of peppery heat.

"I'm sorry I didn't cook," she told him. "That would have meant a trip to the grocery store, and I was already running late."

"A career woman can't do it all."

Was that a simple statement of fact or a criticism? Wanting the evening to go well, she decided to deem it non-antagonistic.

"But —" he wiped a drip of duck sauce from the

corner of his mouth, "—a phone call would have been nice. To let me know you were coming home."

"I come home every night."

"Not early enough for dinner." The crispy spring roll cracked when he sank his teeth into it.

"Well, that's true," she admitted.

"I don't like to complain. But I spent more time with you when I lived over in Holly Oaks."

The apartment complex where he used to live was several miles outside of town and Lauren had made a special effort to visit him there at least once a week for dinner or a movie outing.

"Dad, I see you every morning."

He snorted, crumpling his paper napkin in the palm of his hand. "Yeah, for two or three minutes. Long enough to say hello and good-bye."

"That's not true." But even as she said the words, she knew it was. She forced all of the defensiveness out of her tone when she said, "Come on, Dad. Let's not fight."

"Do you know it's been almost three weeks since we sat down to a meal together?"

"No way—"

"Has, too." He ripped open a second packet of duck sauce and squirted a liberal amount onto his roll. "You know what your problem is, Lauren?

You're too independent. You don't need anyone. It isn't healthy to isolate yourself too much."

Lauren nearly choked on a water chestnut. She'd finally gotten up the nerve to approach her dad about how he chose to live his life, brought home Chinese food for a nice, cozy dinner during which she planned to have her discussion with him, and she was the one being preached at.

"You've never needed me," he said.

Her knee-jerk reaction was to disagree, but before she could he barreled full-steam ahead.

"You didn't need Greg, either. Not really."

She lowered her hand. "Not needing Greg turned out to be a good thing, I'd say."

"Honey, did you ever think that that might be why your marriage didn't work out?"

His hazel eyes held not a hint of unkindness. But even though his words were soft, they jabbed at her as sharply as if he'd used his chopsticks.

"Why does every conversation have to come down to Greg and our divorce? Dad, Greg and I are history. You're going to have to get used to that."

"I am. I am," he assured her. "I'm just worried about you, is all. I'm afraid that if you keep up this—" he waved his hands in the air "—staunch independence, you're going to live the rest of your life alone."

"'Staunch independence'?" She parroted him, sarcasm tinting the words ever so slightly. "You make me sound like a defecting country."

"Don't be angry. I'm only trying to help you."

For some reason that only annoyed her further. "Independence isn't a bad thing. Most fathers want to raise daughters who are self-reliant."

He paused, the flaps of the rice box he'd picked up hanging open. "I didn't raise you, Lauren. Not really." He rested his forearms on the edge of the table and looked at her intently. "I was in the house, yes. I earned the money and paid the bills. But the day your mother died, you went from being a little girl to a grown woman."

Lauren couldn't breathe. He had just described exactly how she had felt as a teen. But she'd never imagined that he had realized it.

"You came home from school and cleaned the house. You shopped for groceries. You cooked the meals. You turned into the homemaker of the year. You attacked the job with such single-mindedness that I had to come up with some pretty inventive ways to get you away from it from time to time." His small smile was cut short by a deep, drawn-out sigh. "I guess it was my fault. I should have stepped up to the plate. I should have been the leader. But all that planning and organizing you did, I don't know... it gave you something to do. Gave you a place to focus your energy. I thought it was a good thing at the time. It helped you to, you know, get through the heartache of losing your mother."

His shoulders rounded, and Lauren felt the tension inside her release. Sadness seemed to surround them any time they discussed the tragedy they have faced together all those years ago.

As a teen in the steely grips of grief, she'd decided she couldn't ever depend on anyone besides herself. She could remember the day, the very moment, in fact, that she had come to the morbid conclusion. The house had been empty and deathly quiet when she had rushed in from school, gasping for breath, tears of humiliation streaming down her face. A group of 'popular' girls had teased her about her budding breasts showing through her t-shirt. You need a bra, a teacher had taken her aside and curtly advised. But Lauren knew nothing about bras, and the idea of talking to her father about buying underwear mortified her.

That had been the instant that she realized she had to do for herself. She'd been so upset that her mother had been taken away from her, that she'd been left to deal with these problems on her own. It wasn't fair that her mom had gone away and left her to struggle with dirty dishes and dust bunnies and bra buying. But deal with them she would, she'd resolved.

"Your mother was the strong one."

Her dad's voice nudged her back to the present.

"You know it and I know it. She held us together as a family, Lauren. I guess I should have stopped you from stepping into her shoes, but... " His voice trailed and he lifted a shoulder. Then he shook his head. "I'm afraid I did you a great disservice when I—"

"Oh, Dad, no," she whispered. She leaned forward, slid her hand over his forearm. "Don't ever say that. Don't even think it. Your letting me take charge was good for me. That experience made me a very strong person."

He nodded, but it wasn't in happy agreement. "Too strong to let anyone else into your life. Too strong to be half of a couple. You and Greg were married, but the two of you seemed to live separate lives." Worry clouded his gaze. "I know that you're through with Greg. I don't agree with it. Don't like it at all. But I can see what's in front of my face."

He swallowed, looking miserable. "Lauren, honey, I don't want you to spend your whole life alone."

Lauren had no idea he'd been troubled. That he'd been worried about her. All this time she'd thought he was angry with her. Disappointed in her that her marriage had failed.

She didn't know how to appease his anxiety. But he'd given her an opening; an opportunity so good that not taking it would be plain wrong. She took the steamed rice from him and spooned some onto his plate. "Funny you should say that." She arranged the other take out containers so they were wide open and within his reach. "I've been thinking the same thing about you lately."

Her dad sat back in his chair, his arms lowering to his sides, saying nothing.

"Norma Jean's been coming around, I noticed," she began. "She happened to mention to me that she's been calling you."

The tension in her father's expression eased. Then a smile shadowed the corners of his mouth, his eyes shining.

"She said she asked you out. More than once."

"Oh." He waved his hand. "She didn't mean anything." He reached for the box of beef. "She was just being nice to an old man."

"That's not what I'm hearing. She's honestly interested."

Her dad dipped his chin nearly to his chest, his cheeks flushing red. "Lauren, Norma Jean is a lovely lady, but she's too young for me."

Lauren grinned. "She doesn't think so."

He splashed soy sauce onto the beef and broccoli, then snapped the bottle closed and set it on the table. "Honey, your mother was the love of my life. She was perfect. In every way. And we were good together. Real good. Something like that doesn't come along but once in a lifetime."

Hearing him voice his loyalty to her mother melted Lauren's heart. The love they had shared had been real and true. There had been a time when she would have used those very words to describe her relationship with Greg. Real and true love.

"From the moment I met your mother," her father said softly, "I felt I couldn't live without her."

Misty emotion sparkled in his eyes and Lauren reached over and curled her fingertips into his palm.

It was odd that Greg would come into her mind so vividly now. When they had first begun dating, one of the reasons she had fallen in love with him was not because he couldn't live without her, but because he could. Greg had his own hopes and dreams and goals. He'd been working with his father in the hardware store back then, and he'd had his budding carpentry business, too. He'd seemed happy to give her the space she'd needed to finish her education. Even after they married, he hadn't been one to hover. She'd felt free to work whatever hours she felt necessary to get her practice going. There had been dinners with clients, networking meetings, seminars, conferences. And Greg had never given her any flak. He'd had his interests and she'd had hers, and it had worked for them.

For a time, anyway.

Lauren wondered about the charge her father had made about her being too independent, too strong. Could she have had it all wrong all those years? Could Greg have needed more from her? If she'd been more involved in her marriage, spent more time with her husband, could they have avoided the pitfalls that had tripped them up?

"Don't go all melancholy on me, now."

Her father squeezed her fingers affectionately,

and she blinked her way out of the past. This show of tenderness was rare for Lew Hunkavic.

"Does it make you unhappy when I talk about your mother?" he asked.

"Oh, no," she assured him, straightening in the chair and picking up her chopsticks once again. "I love hearing how much the two of you loved each other." She poked at the vegetables on her plate, sorting through her cluttered thoughts to get back to the subject at hand. "Dad, going out to dinner with Norma Jean wouldn't mean you're betraying Mom, or what the two of you had together."

"Aw, now Lauren." A piece of broccoli disappeared between his lips and he chewed.

"Listen to me for a minute, would you? You need to get out of this house. You sit here day in and day out, doing nothing—"

"I do plenty."

"Don't get mad," she told him, smiling. Then she teased, "I listened to your observations about my life without giving you lip."

He went quiet, but it was clear that he didn't like it.

"You might have fun with Norma Jean," she said. "It's good to have friends. She's someone to do things with. Go places with." She lifted a mushroom slice between her chopsticks. "You've been alone for a long time, Dad."

"Okay, okay," he said gruffly. "Are we done now?"

"We are if you promise me that you'll at least think about accepting Norma's offer."

He sighed as he scooped up a forkful of beef and rice. "I'll think about it."

She smiled. "Good."

"If you'll think about what I said."

Sliding the soft mushroom into her mouth, she nodded. She suddenly felt all warm inside. It was nice to know that her father loved her, worried about her. He really did care.

His empty fork was poised over his plate. "I am glad to see that you're softening just a little here lately."

She just looked at him, completely baffled by the statement.

"Your blood boiled because Greg gave away his time, helped some people for free—" he stirred rich, brown sauce into his rice "—and now you're doing the same thing."

Lauren balanced the chopsticks on the edge of her dinner plate and picked up her glass of wine. "What are you talking about?"

"Norma Jean told me all about it." He chuckled and chewed. "You've hired that Shaw boy to work out at the barn so he can earn back the money his daddy paid you. If that's not doling out charity, I don't know what is."

Her spine went rigid and she nearly sloshed wine onto the tablecloth. "It's not the same thing at all."

"Ah, ah, ah." He waggled his finger at her. "Don't give me lip for making an observation."

The deep rumble of his laughter had her glowering at him over the rim of her glass.

Oh, yeah. He loved her. He worried. He cared.

But he still enjoyed getting in the last dig.

Chapter Eleven

It is only the wisest and the stupidest
that cannot change.
~Confucius

"**I** don't want to see you in my courtroom again, young man," the judge said. "Do you understand?"

"Yes, sir." Scott Shaw, Jr. nodded sharply. "I'll stay out of trouble. I promise."

"I'm going to hold you to that, Mr. Shaw. And if you break that promise, you'll be one very sorry pup." Judge Owens smacked her gavel against the sound block. "This court is adjourned."

Lauren gathered her paperwork and tapped it on the tabletop.

"Thanks, Ms. Flynn," Scott, Jr. said. "I'm grateful for all your help. And your advice. I-I can't believe I thought about coming to court without you."

The sincere appreciation the young man expressed had Lauren shooting him a smile.

Scott's father approached them from where he'd been sitting in the gallery seating. "Lauren, what did the judge mean about moving Scotty's case? I mean, Scott's case. Does this mean his trouble's not over?"

"It's over as long as he doesn't find any more. Trouble, that is. Judge Owens moved the case to the Stet Docket." Lauren slid the papers into her briefcase and snapped it shut. "It's a docket of inactive cases." She started for the door and both Scott and his son fell into step with her. She looked at the younger Shaw to her right. "Your case will remain on the docket for a year. If you keep your nose clean, this will all go away for good."

The teen fisted both hands and raised them overhead like a winning prize fighter as his father held open the door of the courtroom.

"If you break the law," Lauren warned, "any law, the penalty for disturbing the peace and resisting arrest will be added on top of any other penalties or punishment you might incur."

Scott lowered his hands to his sides and his smile waned.

Lauren jabbed the elevator call button. "Yes. It's that serious. You'd better mind your Ps and Qs, Scott."

"I will. I will."

The three of them stepped into the elevator and the doors slid closed.

"You were amazing in there," Scott, Sr. told her. "Your arguments made it seem like carrying that blow-up contraption down Main Street was the most logical thing in the world for Scotty to do."

"Just doing my job." Lauren shifted her briefcase from one hand to the other.

Scott looked at his son, his mouth flattening soberly. "Scotty... Scott, you need to stay out of trouble, son. I mean it."

Lauren was happy that Scott was taking her advice to heart. He was trying to break the habit of juvenilizing his son's name.

"I will, Dad," the teen said solemnly. Then his whole demeanor changed when he grinned at Lauren. "I couldn't believe it when you challenged that dude to admit he'd like to have a five foot penis of his own to parade up Main Street. And you did it without cracking a smile. I thought his head was going to implode."

"That 'dude' was an Assistant State's Attorney," she told him. "I'm sure he didn't appreciate my making him look a fool in front of the judge, and that certainly wasn't my plan, but he was going on as if you were some kind of ax murderer instead of a college kid who'd made a simple mistake." She tucked an errant strand of hair behind her ear. "I'd have never gotten away with that had we been in any other courtroom besides Judge Owens'. A male judge would have called me on the carpet, I'm sure."

The doors of the elevator slid open and they stepped out into the hall.

"Dad, I gotta run," Scott said.

His father looked disappointed. "I thought I'd take everyone to lunch. To celebrate."

"I have class. Sorry." The young man looked at Lauren. "Thanks again. For everything."

"You're welcome, Scott. You're working at the barn on Saturday?"

"Sure thing," he said and then took off toward the front entrance in a loping trot.

Lauren's gaze was drawn from Scott to the

double glass doors beyond him where a tall, red-haired woman entered the courthouse. She looked awfully familiar, and when she lifted her face, Lauren smiled. Jo Leigh Stapleton stopped to peruse the large index board hanging in the vestibule.

"Well, well, well," Scott Sr. said in a smooth, sing-song tone, "looks like it's just you and me for lunch, Ms. Flynn. What do you say? Can I take you across the street to the diner for a little celebration?"

When Lauren looked into his handsome face his blue eyes were flashing with delightful anticipation.

"Scott, I'm sorry." She darted a glance at her watch. "I've got to get back to the office."

Over Scott's shoulder, she watched Jo Leigh head for the staircase that led to the basement.

"Lauren, I have to confess that I can't figure you out. I've never had this much trouble reading a woman before. She likes me, she doesn't like me. I feel the urge to buy a daisy and start plucking the petals to try to find an answer." The humor tingeing his voice didn't quite cover his hurt feelings.

She had sent him mixed signals. She'd smiled in

response to his compliments, and their flirtatious banter had been nothing but pure fun. He'd made her feel good about herself again; he'd made her feel desirable.

"Scott, I'm really sorry. I tried to explain that I didn't think it was a good idea for us to go out while I was representing your son." But after working at the barn with him she'd had the feeling that he might be just the man she needed to help her move on with her life. So why was she still ducking his advances and turning down his invitations?

"The case is over."

She nodded. "It is." Something kept her from saying more, and she was at a loss to figure out what it was.

His words were clipped when he asked, "Can I at least walk you back to your office?"

Lauren grimaced apologetically. "I'm sorry, but I just saw an old friend head downstairs and I want to go say hello." She took a backward step into the waiting elevator and hit the button marked B. "But I have your number."

He brightened; clearly, he hadn't expected to hear her say that. "You'll call me?"

Before she could answer, the elevator doors whispered shut.

* * *

"Hey, lady," Lauren said, coming up behind the tall redhead, "you look lost."

Jo Leigh whirled around to face her. "Lauren!" They hugged, and Jo Leigh whispered, "You look great."

"So do you."

The woman smiled her thanks and then admitted, "I am lost."

"This courthouse is my second home. Maybe I can point you in the right direction."

"I want to apply for a business license."

Lauren pointed down the east wing. "Licensing and Permits. Third door on the left."

"Thanks, thanks. So how have you been?"

"I'm well, thanks." But her smile felt suddenly plastic. What else could she say? My husband made some financial decisions that nearly put me in poor house? I was so pissed I filed for divorce? My dad's moved in with me? I've been flying solo for so long I've forgotten what it's like to get naked with a man?

"I've been doing just fine, Jo Leigh. How about yourself?"

"I'm great, Lauren. Just great." Jo Leigh hitched her purse strap up onto her shoulder. "After Jim died, I thought my life was over."

Lauren reached out and touched her friend's forearm. "I heard about Jim. I'm sorry."

Appreciation shined in Jo Leigh's eyes. "But things have really turned around for me and Tracy. She's my daughter. We're doing well." Her smile broadened. "I'm starting a business, Lauren. A day care center. I'm going with a bumblebee theme. I'm calling the place Babee Day Care." With a well-practiced reach, she slid her fingers into a side pocket of her purse and then thrust a business card at Lauren. "With two e's instead of a y. See?"

A fat, animated black and yellow striped bee smiled from the upper left corner of the card, and bold, block lettering spelled out the name of the day care.

"Cute," Lauren exclaimed.

"This is my dream, Lauren. Something I've always wanted to do." Jo Leigh's smile grew even bigger, if that were possible. "And Greg is helping me do it. This wouldn't be happening if it weren't for him."

Lauren nodded. "He told me he was doing some work for you."

Jo Leigh looked relieved. "I think it's great that you two are on speaking terms. So many divorced couples aren't, you know?" She flashed another smile. "Anyway, Greg's renovating my three car garage. Giving it a real overhaul. He put in duct work for heat and air conditioning and insulation and drywall."

A funny feeling nudged at Lauren. Greg had told her he was merely putting in some cabinets at Jo Leigh's. Why would he downplay the important role he'd taken in getting her business off the ground?

"He even installed a powder room, Lauren. He is such a talented guy." Palpable excitement rolled off Jo Leigh and she looked about ready to hop up and down right where she stood. "And I'm getting all this for free. Can you believe it?"

Lauren couldn't have been more stunned had she taken an unexpected punch to the diaphragm. Inhaling was difficult; responding was impossible.

The tinny elevator bell rang. The doors slid open and half a dozen people exited onto the basement level. The two women had to slide to one side of the hallway and the much needed distraction gave Lauren a few seconds to gather her wits. No wonder Greg hadn't been more forthcoming with her about his job at Jo Leigh's. Once again, his priorities were skewed. Sure, Jo Leigh could use some help. Life had to be hard for a widow starting a new business, but couldn't he have charged her less than his normal fee rather than not charging her at all? This kind of behavior was exactly what got him into trouble to begin with. Would the man never learn?

When they were once again alone in the hallway, Jo Leigh said, "Listen, Lauren, Greg told me that your divorce was final."

Lauren nodded, the corners of her mouth tightening. Everyone in the entire world seemed to view divorce as an awful thing, an event that required some sort of condolence speech that was usually followed by words of encouragement. Since taking Greg to court, every friend and colleague she met wanted to commiserate with her. She braced herself for Jo Leigh's expression of sympathy.

Jo Leigh met her gaze. "Would you mind if he and I see each other?"

* * *

"She was a friend of mine back in high school," Lauren explained to Norma Jean. "She'd come to the courthouse to apply for a business license."

Clients had been waiting when Lauren returned to the office so she hadn't been able to tell Norma how she'd unexpectedly met up with Jo Leigh until now. Glancing at the clock, she saw it was officially 'after business hours.'

Norma slid a file into the cabinet drawer and closed it. "What kind of business?"

"A day care center. She was so excited." Lauren's brow tensed as her gaze trailed to the far side of the room. "Jo Leigh looked good. She really did."

She looked better than good, Lauren decided. She looked happy. Ecstatic, really. During their conversation Jo Leigh couldn't stop smiling.

"Lauren, sweetheart."

She blinked her way out of a thoughtful fog.

"You're saying all the right words about this friend—" Norma Jean teasingly tapped her index finger against her jaw "—but why does my gut tell me you're not really feeling it?"

The quip was meant to make her smile, but Lauren couldn't seem to rustle one up.

"Greg lied, Norma Jean," she said. She explained how Greg's version of the work he was doing for Jo Leigh didn't jive with what she'd learned this afternoon.

After hearing Lauren out, confusion flattened

Norma Jean's mouth. "Why do you care what Greg is or isn't doing for this woman?"

Lauren shook her head. "It's not that." At least, Lauren hoped it wasn't. No, no, she was sure it wasn't. "Jo Leigh said she's getting, and I quote, 'all this for free.'"

The words chafed like course-grit sandpaper.

Immediately, Norma seemed to understand her feelings; her head tilted and her shoulders sagged as she tucked her hands into her lap.

"I thought the bankruptcy had taught him a lesson," Lauren said, quietly. "I thought losing the hardware store had changed him, Norma Jean. He lost everything. His business, his home, his marriage. Everything." Myriad emotions had her shaking her head slowly from side to side and she couldn't say if it was sadness or irritation. "The man is willing to live in a barn so that he can give away his talent. It just doesn't make sense to me."

"I thought you made him move out of the barn."

"I did, I did." Lauren pulled a pencil from the cup on her desk, shaking her head. "I was just making a point. He told me he'd found a place to live, but for all I know he's living in his truck."

"Oh, he wouldn't do that." The phone rang and Norma Jean held up her index finger. "Hold on just a sec while I get that." She slipped out into the reception area.

The yellow pencil twirled as Lauren slowly rolled it between her flattened palms. Norma was probably right. Greg wouldn't live in his truck. But then Lauren would never have guessed that he'd stoop to living in a barn.

It ticked her off royally to learn that he was continuing to work for free. Sure, he'd always had a big heart. Had always gone out of his way to help people in need. Helping people was all well and good, but he should consider his own well-being, his own financial security, his own future.

She stuffed the pencil back into the cup. No matter where he was living, no matter what choices he made for his business and career, she had to remember it wasn't her problem anymore. He wasn't her problem.

Planting her hands on the armrests and pushing out of her chair, she stalked to the window and stared across the twilit parking lot without actually seeing a thing.

"Would you mind if he and I see each other?"

The question had stunned Lauren. She'd hemmed and stammered, all the while attempting to deal with the emotion that had exploded inside her.

She'd been chatting with Jo Leigh, seeing her as a long lost friend, and suddenly the woman turned into some kind of rival right before her eyes. Lauren had felt covetous and wary, and she couldn't figure out if she was jealous of Jo Leigh, or if she was angry and hurt that Greg was casting aside all the years they'd had together to march forward into a future that no longer included her.

The conglomeration of ugly emotion had swelled inside her like a huge, unmanageable balloon until she'd become completely unnerved. Finally, she'd offered Jo Leigh a tight smile and assured the woman that she and Greg could do as they pleased.

But the flare of utter commotion she'd experienced had shocked her, overwhelmed her, and it continued to completely discombobulate her even now.

She was the one who had asked Greg to move out. She'd been the one to press for a divorce. It was what she'd wanted, dammit. She didn't care if he was seeing other women. Why shouldn't he? He was as free as a bird. As free of her as she was of him.

So why had Jo Leigh's question sent her reeling?

The mere implications filled Lauren's thoughts with thick, gray storm clouds. She didn't want to think about it—refused to think about it. In fact, there was nothing to think about.

Turning away from the window, she marched over to the file cabinet and tugged open the draw labeled S-T. Her fingers walked determinedly across the plastic tabs until she came to Scott Shaw's file. She pulled out the manila folder and flipped through the forms and pages of handwritten notes until she found what she was looking for.

Scott's father's contact information.

"You okay? You still need to talk?" Norma Jean breezed back into her office.

Lauren palmed the business card, surreptitiously sliding it into the pocket of her trousers and then returning the Shaw file where it belonged before shutting the drawer.

Now why would she do that? Why sneak around about calling Scott? Norma Jean was her friend. One of her biggest supporters. She'd be the first one to shout a happy cheer when she heard that Lauren was going to contact the man.

This atypical behavior was freaking her out. But

not enough to have her opening up to Norma about her plans.

"I'm good," she told Norma. "I'm fine. Thanks for listening. I'm totally over it. If Greg doesn't earn another penny in his lifetime, it's a-okay with me." Changing the subject entirely, she asked, "Who was on the phone?"

Norma reached up and tugged at the short wisps of hair behind her ear, her brown eyes shining. "That was Lew. I called him at lunch today and invited him to come with me to the Boys and Girls Club tomorrow. You know I volunteer there a couple of Saturdays a month. They've set up a new computer center and need people to come in to show the kids how to operate them. I thought that would be right up your dad's alley."

Lauren's broad smile was totally genuine. "It is right up his alley, Norma. What a great idea."

"And if we were to stop for pancakes on the way, that wouldn't constitute a date or anything. We'd just be grabbing breakfast, right?" She flashed Lauren a quick wink. "I'll get that man to go out with me one way or another."

"I don't know, Norma. I told him he should get out of the house more, but he's never listened to me in the past."

"Well, he'll listen to me." Norma settled her hands on her trim hips. "I'll liven him up all right. All he needs is a good roll in the hay."

Lauren's eyes bugged. "Norma!" Laughing, she comically clamped her hands over her ears. "I don't want to hear that."

Norma grinned. "Oh, grow up, Lauren," she teased. "Old people do it, too. Heck, we probably do it more than young people. Well, maybe not more than young people, but definitely more than middle-aged people."

Reflecting on her own sexual habits, or lack thereof, Lauren was forced to admit, "Now that I believe." After a moment, she said, "If anyone can get Dad out of the house, Norma, I'd lay odds on you. I think you should know, Dad's a sucker for pancakes."

A beacon wouldn't have outshined Norma Jean's smile. "See there? My instincts were entirely correct about the man." They chuckled and then she said, "If we're all through for the day, Lauren, I'm going to head home. It's been a long week. I'm going to soak in the tub and make an early night of it. I need a good night's sleep if I'm going to tackle your dad in the morning."

"I hope you don't mean that literally," Lauren

joked. "He's got a bad knee." She gave the air a tiny swipe. "You go ahead. I'll lock up here."

Once she was alone in the office, Lauren tidied up. She put away the code books she'd pulled from the bookcase for research earlier in the day. She checked her electronic calendar to see which court dates were scheduled for the beginning of the next week and slid those files into her briefcase so she could read them over the weekend. She was digging in her purse for her keys when Jo Leigh's voice floated through her brain yet again.

"Would you mind...?"

Heat flushed through her body and an odd array of emotions gathered in her chest. Conflicting emotions. Powerful emotions.

Images flooded into her mind unbidden. Pressing her fingertips to her temples, she rubbed rough, tiny circles but could not scrub away the memory of her and Greg's very first meeting.

The sun had beat down like a hammer that hot August day. She was home from college for the summer. Her pre-law degree was behind her and she had scored well on the LSATs. She'd been accepted at three of the five schools of law she'd applied to. Everything was right with the world.

She'd gone to a friend's house for a day of

lounging by the pool. A handful of college girls were there, all in skin-baring bikinis, all full of talk focused on nothing but career plans and life goals. These women were serious about the future.

Her friend's parents had hired a carpenter to repair the door to the pool house which had been sticking. The other girls had taken little notice of the dark-haired, dark-eyed young man who was sweating in the blaring heat. Well, that wasn't quite true. They noticed him, but not a single one of them was interested in a man who worked with his hands, who wore blue jeans and work boots on the job.

But there was something about the way Greg moved, about the way he'd handled that plane, his fingertips gliding, probing, checking the wood with each pass of the tool that caught Lauren's attention. She'd watched him work, saw the meticulous care he put into the job, her gaze hidden behind a chic pair of large sunglasses.

The summer sun pounded the concrete surrounding the pool. Beads of sweat had formed on her chest, rolled down her belly, and she'd been wearing next to nothing. She could only imagine how hot Greg must have been in his cotton t-shirt, denim pants and heavy work boots. She'd risen from the lounge chair and grabbed an icy bottle of water from the cooler. Her friends had gaped in disbelief as she'd padded across the cement expanse and offered the fix-it guy a drink.

Their conversation had been so short and inane that it was nothing but forgettable. But he'd appreciated her effort; that she did remember. Gratitude had shown in the black depths of his eyes. She'd headed to her lounge chair and he'd stopped her with a soft, "Hey."

She remembered turning back to face him.

"Would you let me take you to dinner some time?" he'd asked.

"Yeah," she'd told him. Oh, yeah.

And then he'd smiled.

Lauren scrubbed her hands over her face, brushed her bangs from her damp forehead.

"No, Lauren," she said to herself, right out loud. She repeated the word even more firmly before adding, "You don't mind if Greg and Jo Leigh see each other."

She pulled the business card from her pocket and placed it on her desktop. The small rectangle of stiff, cream-colored paper stood out starkly against the rich cherry wood.

She'd put Scott off long enough. It was time to

jump back into the dating fray. She picked up the phone, punched in the numbers and listened to the ring on the other end of the line.

Greg was moving on with his life. She shouldn't be bothered by that. She wouldn't be bothered by that. It was normal. Natural.

It was time for her to do the same.

Chapter Twelve

How many of you have ever started dating because
you were too lazy to commit suicide?
-Judy Tenuta

The hem of the slinky dress struck her several inches above the knee and revealed her shapely calves. The fitted style showed off her slender waist and the red fabric made her skin glow. Lauren turned to the side, scrutinizing her image in the full-length mirror that hung on the back of her bedroom door. The material clung to her butt and her flat tummy and accentuated her breasts. Facing forward with enough momentum to make the skirt dance around her thighs, she studied her upper body; the spaghetti straps drew attention to her slender shoulders, and the same key-hole opening that prevented her from wearing a bra highlighted her cleavage.

It was a great dress. A sexy dress. A dress that would surely turn a man's head.

And practically beg him to make love to her.

Lauren groaned in frustration, yanking down the back zipper, stepping out of the cherry confection and tossing it onto the bed.

There was nothing she wouldn't love more than a night filled with sensuous pleasure, but that was no message to be sending Scott on their very first night out together. It was no way to start what could very well turn out to be a budding relationship... a relationship that just might prove to be something meaningful.

Half the clothes she owned were in a jumble on the bed. Lauren went to the closet and perused what was left. She tugged a black, knee-length pencil skirt from its hanger, and once she'd donned it, she chose a lacy bra and then a plain, white blouse. She was fastening the last button when she turned back to the mirror.

She looked like a librarian... or a lawyer on her way to court. Heaving a sigh, she yanked her way out of the outfit and pitched it on top of the ever growing pile on the bed.

What was the matter with her?

She sat down on the bed and propped her chin up with her fist, ready for a good sulk, her hair cascading over her shoulder.

She knew good and well what was wrong. She was scared spitless. She hadn't been on a date with anyone other than Greg in...

Dear Lord, just how long had it been?

Her mind worked out the numbers backward. Separated a year, married twelve, and she'd dated Greg exclusively for four years before their wedding.

Seventeen years. She'd been a kid then.

How were adults supposed to act on a date?

Wincing at her reflection, she muttered, "Don't be stupid."

How hard could it be? You meet at a restaurant, you eat a little, you talk a little, you laugh a little, and before you know it the date will be over.

"It won't even get started," she grumbled, "if you don't choose something to wear."

Lauren dragged herself back to the closet. She pulled out a dress that was years old but Audrey-Hepburn-classic. The silk was such a deep purple that it almost appeared black. She slid the cocktail dress over her head and it whispered down her body.

Taking this first step out into the dating world was as logical as it was necessary. If her dad was right about her being 'too independent', then going out with Scott could be the answer to her problem. Or at least the beginning of an answer. If there was an answer. She wasn't sure there was a problem. Chuckling at her confusion, she made short work of the dress's zipper and went to the mirror.

Perfect. The dress looked nice. Elegant and simple. Flattering to her figure without being overtly sexy. The dress really was perfect for a first date, but she'd ask for a second opinion from her dad before she left.

One pair of black, open-toed heels and a black clutch later, she was ready to roll. She paused a second or two to comb her fingers through her hair and check her makeup.

"I hope you know what you're doing," she mouthed to the nervous blonde looking back at her in the mirror. She feared she was so rusty at this dating thing that she really wasn't sure what she was getting into. She'd have to muddle through even though that wasn't her normal style. On the job, she liked to plan her actions and choreograph her words, but that wasn't possible when she was heading into such unknown territory.

Dating was not a foreign land, she reminded herself firmly. She'd be fine.

On a final deep sigh, she headed out the door of her bedroom. The wardrobe mess would have to wait until later.

Her father was snoring softly in his old green easy chair while the anchorman droned on about one of the local sports teams. Norma Jean and the kids at the Boys and Girls Club must have worn him out today. He'd enjoyed himself, Lauren had been able to tell that when he'd arrived home this afternoon even though he'd complained about the children's lack of manners.

Just as well that he was napping. He wouldn't have liked the idea that she was going out. With a man. Other than Greg. Oh, he'd told her he realized she and Greg were through. He'd even told her he didn't want her spending her life alone. But he'd have given her grief. Even when she tried to act on his advice he groused. A lifetime of being his daughter had taught her as much. He couldn't fight who he was.

Lauren jotted a quick note and set it on top of

the remote where he couldn't help but see it when he woke, and then she picked up her keys.

"Night, Dad," she whispered, nerves jitterbugging in her stomach as she shut the front door behind her.

* * *

"So what do you have over there?" she asked, peering across the candlelit table at Scott's plate.

"Let's see." He used his fork to sort through the salad. "Lettuce, roasted beets, candied walnuts and crumbles of blue cheese. It's good." Then he chuckled. "There's a woman who works for me, Gail... she'd swell up like a balloon if she ate this cheese. She's allergic." He snickered again and then shoveled another bite of salad into his mouth.

Lauren wasn't sure where to go with that comment so she fell silent and munched on peppery arugula and wild mushrooms that had been decoratively arranged on her salad plate.

"You see Scott today?" he asked.

"I did. He came to the barn just as I was leaving. I don't know how long he stayed." Lauren scooted a baby carrot to the edge of her plate. "The guy stopped by, too. The one who's going to airbrush the animals. He was really nice. Knowledgeable, too. We settled on a price for his work—a great price, I'm happy to say. And he took one of the horses with him. To his studio. Promised he'd bring it back next week."

A smile and a nod was Scott's only response, then he focused on his plate again.

Small talk. People engaged in it every day. All that was needed were two individuals and an interesting subject to volley back and forth. The range of topics was as wide as the great, blue sky. Art. Entertainment. Culture. Sports. Fashion. The list was endless. Lauren had never thought of herself as verbally clumsy, yet she was having an awful time sustaining a simple discussion tonight.

All around her, she heard the murmur of lively conversations taking place between patrons of Charlie's. The upscale eatery had opened back in the summer on Sterling's up and coming east side. Lauren had heard about it from the same source that provided her with all the town news; Norma Jean. The restaurant marketed itself as specializing in 'New American cuisine with Old World charm.' And, indeed, charm pervaded the place. Candlelight glowed against the richly painted stucco walls and soft strains of jazz floated on air thick with ambiance. With food this delicious and atmosphere this cozy and relaxed, Lauren should have been having a good time. But if she were pressed for the truth, she'd have to say otherwise.

The problem, it seemed, was that she and Scott had little to talk about, or else neither of them were very adept in the fine art of making small talk. Oh, they'd tried. Both of them had. And the realization that conversation between them continued to fall flat with each attempt had her feeling self-conscious. Lauren had come to the conclusion that, workaholics that they were, she and Scott focused too much attention on their jobs and not enough time reading the classics or listening to good music or seeing the latest blockbusters.

She and Scott had done just fine together during those short bursts of time they had previously spent together; at her office or in court. During those times, the conversation had focused mainly on Scott's son and the court case. They'd had a great time that Saturday morning they'd been at the barn together. Lauren didn't remember feeling the least bit awkward and had actually enjoyed hearing about what Scott did for a living. It might sound silly, but she wondered if it was possible that they could have talked themselves out in that short time they were together that day?

She placed her fork across her salad plate, then

leaned back to pick up the linen napkin from her lap. The fabric was stiff against her mouth. Then she tucked the napkin back into place and smiled, gearing up to venture another try.

"This place is great, isn't it?"

Scott nodded. "Did I tell you the owner hired my firm to handle their insurance?"

"Yes. Yes, you did." Lauren fought the sigh building in the back of her throat. He'd told her twice in the thirty minutes they'd been in the bar having cocktails.

"Did I tell you Charlie's is my account? My people are handling it."

Lauren nodded, just as proud that she was able to hold her smile in place as he was that he'd won the restaurant owner's business.

"The owners are offering their full-time employees—"

An excellent package, she silently provided.

"—an excellent package. Their part-timers aren't faring too badly either."

Her eyes nearly crossed as Scott launched into a drawn-out explanation of HMOs and PPOs and the monotonous minutia that made the entities different. Shoot me now, she thought miserably, please, somebody, just shoot me now.

Some part of her brain turned inward, searching desperately for a reprieve, and took a nosedive into the deep pool of memories of when she and Greg had dated.

The first time he'd taken her out, they'd had a blast. He'd refused to tell her where they were going. His black eyes had danced and the air of excitement that had filled the cab of his beat up truck had made her feel light-hearted.

"It'll be an adventure," he'd promised. "Trust me."

She had, and she hadn't regretted it for a moment.

Riding a horse had been a new experience for her. And judging from the trouble Greg had had staying in the saddle, he hadn't been much of an equestrian, either. They had bounced and laughed all the way across the meadow and up the wooded path to the top of the hill where they had tethered the horses and enjoyed the wine and cheese and fresh, crusty bread that Greg had packed.

That day was emblazoned in her memory. A cool breeze had kicked up to take some of the stifling heat out of the summer air. The sky had turned a full palate of varying hues as the sun dipped lower toward the horizon. The glorious mantle above them had looked something close to a miracle and left them speechless all the way back to the stable.

Something close to a miracle? Okay, so maybe her imagination had toyed with the memory a tad.

"Ah, so you've had this experience, I see."

She scrabbled her way back into the here and now, panic billowing in her chest. "I beg your pardon?"

Scott's smiled slipped the smallest fraction. "You grinned," he said. "I figured that meant you'd been confused, too. You know, over which health benefits to opt in or out of."

Lauren nodded, lifted her hands. "Who hasn't?"

"Exactly. I'm trying hard to simplify the language, the forms, everything."

"What an excellent idea," Lauren breathed, thankful that she'd made an adequate recovery and silently vowing to pay closer attention to the conversation.

Later as Scott walked her to her car, she stifled a yawn. It felt like midnight, yet when she glanced at her watch, she was surprised to see that they'd been inside Charlie's less than two hours.

"I screwed this up, didn't I?" He settled his palm low on her back. "I talked about work too much."

"Don't be silly." The warmth of him seeped through the silk fabric of her dress. "It was fine."

He rolled his eyes at her choice of words.

"It was great," she quickly amended, stopping by her driver's side door. When she saw skepticism continued to cloud his blue gaze, she expounded, "I had fun, Scott."

The reassurance made him smile.

"Can we do this again?" he asked, inching toward her.

She smiled. "I'd like that." The pathway to hell was paved with lies, and she could hear Beelzebub laughing hysterically at her, but the truth would only hurt the man's feelings.

Scott reached up and brushed her hair over her shoulder with the back of his hand before leaning in. "Would you mind if I kissed you good-night?"

His whispery breath skittered across the sensitive skin at the curve of her neck. She could smell his cedar-laced cologne, the smooth-shaven skin of his jaw enticing her to reach up for a touch. Lauren took a moment to study his features. He had a nice mouth, expressive eyes that could go from lively to sultry in an instant, and she knew if he were to smile, his cheeks would dimple.

She shook her head, slowly, emphatically. "I

wouldn't mind at all," she murmured and knew without a doubt that she was being completely and utterly honest.

He placed a butterfly kiss on the corner of her mouth, and then another. Then his lips covered hers, warm and soft and moist. He traced a light line up the full length of her neck, the heat from his fingertips sending a shivery cascade over her back and arms. He slid his other hand around behind her and made small, massaging circles on the small of her back. She felt herself relaxing into him, her hips and belly making full contact with his.

Need sprouted deep within her, sensitizing her skin and setting her heart racing.

He teased and tasted her lips with his, and the gentle suction of his mouth against hers made her want to groan. Although he was restrained, this was by no means a chaste kiss. He lingered, gentle and hesitant, as if memorizing the taste of her on his tongue, the feel of her lips on his. He placed one final fleeting kiss on her mouth and broke contact. Then he slid his thumb over her chin, the curve of her jaw.

Lauren opened her eyes slowly, disappointment

leaving her in a quick, breathy exhale. "Wow," she whispered. "That was very nice."

Scott only smiled, but his blue eyes lit with pleasure. He opened her car door for her. "Night," he said before turning and walking away.

* * *

When she let herself into the house, the low murmur of the television told her that her father hadn't yet gone up to bed. She walked into the living room and he lifted a hand in greeting.

"Been taking it easy tonight?" she asked.

He nodded in answer, reaching up to scrub at his broad forehead. "Got a little headache going. I hope I don't have a sinus infection coming on."

"I'll go get you a pain reliever and a glass of water." Lauren took in the newspaper that was piled in disarray on the floor by his chair. She scanned the nearby end table. "Have you been reading the news without your glasses, Dad? The strain of squinting might cause a headache."

He automatically reached up and patted the top of his head where his glasses were often perched, then he searched his lap and the tabletop, too. He scowled, clearly unappreciative of her pointing out that his pain might have nothing to do with his sinuses.

"Found your note," he said, gruffly. After a small pause, he asked, "Went out on a date, eh? You have a good time?"

She sensed he had other, more probing, questions he would rather have asked, but he didn't and she was grateful for that. Tapping her small clutch against her thigh, she contemplated her answer.

Anxiety had her nerves frayed raw before she'd left the house tonight; she'd dreaded the thought of venturing out into the dating world. And with good reason, it turned out. She'd been bored to tears listening to Scott's 'work talk' and she was certain she'd likewise tortured him.

But then they had strolled out into the autumn evening. They had paused by her car for that goodnight kiss. A kiss that had been excruciatingly sweet.

Lauren inhaled deeply and offered her father a bright expression. "You know," she told him, "it wasn't half bad."

Chapter Thirteen

It's been so long since I've made love,
I can't even remember who gets tied up.

~Joan Rivers

"**Y**our Honor, my client, Britney Renee Colbert, is petitioning the court for an Order of Protection against her husband, Robert Walter Colbert, also known as 'Bub' and 'Bubby.'" Lauren stood next to Britney, a woman in her mid-twenties whose wafer-thin body could probably have been knocked over by a stiff wind. "Mr. and Mrs. Colbert have been married for eighteen months and have cohabitated for the entirety of their marriage."

Judge Brooks' expression was kind as he asked,

"Mrs. Colbert, can you tell me the nature of your abuse?"

Britney fidgeted, tugging at the sleeve of her blouse, swiping too-long, mousey brown bangs out of her eyes. The skin on both her boney wrists was banded with sickly shades of yellow. "Sir, my lawyer told me you were gonna want to know what Bubby did to me. I don't want to get him into trouble. I just want him to go see someone. He needs help."

Lauren had coached her client to stick to the facts, had warned her that if she wanted legal protection from the state of Maryland she would have to issue a statement against her husband. The kindness that had softened the judge's mouth only an instant before all but disappeared. Now, he just looked tired.

"Mrs. Colbert, it seems to me you're the one in need of help. I don't have the authority to force your husband to seek counseling or medical treatment, unless you're willing to file a complaint. I'll also issue a writ of protection for you. If and only if you convince me it's warranted."

Britney sighed and lifted her hands beseechingly. "He doesn't drink all the time. Bub is just having a hard time—"

"Mrs. Colbert." Judge Brooks stopped her with an upraised hand. "I'm not interested in hearing about your husband's difficulties. Today, we want to focus on what this court can do for you."

The judge shot Lauren a warning glance and she could only shrug. If Britney refused the legal advice she'd paid for, there was really nothing Lauren could do.

The young woman's jaw jutted to one side. "He wouldn't let me leave the house. But only because I threatened to pack my bags and go for good." Her tone went snippy, as if she was peeved that the legal system was forcing her to tattle on her husband. "I won't have sex with him when he's drinking. I put up with a lot, but that's one thing I put my foot down about. But my rules make him angry when he's had one too many. If he'd just get some help with his drinking. Isn't there anything you can do?"

"I've already explained what I'm able to do." The judge's brows lifted in warning. "Please don't waste this court's time."

It seemed that young Britney's life was swarming with excitement, while Lauren's was anything but. Oh, that kind of commotion wasn't what Lauren was looking for, not by any means. However, it sure would be nice to contemplate an evening out and not face utter tedium.

She and Scott had seen each other six times over the past two weeks and the only thing keeping Lauren interested were the mind-blowing kisses that ended each evening. Those fantasy farewells had grown steamier and more arousing with each successive date. Just thinking about kissing that man was enough to make her pulse thump even now.

"Bubby isn't a waste of time," Britney staunchly asserted.

"If I may, Your Honor," Lauren cut in. Her client needed a little assistance or she wasn't going to get the protection she needed. Lauren reached for the legal pad and pen sitting on the table. "Last Tuesday, Mr. Colbert—" she read from the paper "—shoved and slapped his wife. He bound her hands and ankles together to keep her from leaving their home. After several hours, Mrs. Colbert was able to free herself and fled to the local women's shelter. The following day, Mr. Colbert went to the shelter, and when Mrs. Colbert refused to see him, he rammed his truck into the front door. The police were called and Mr. Colbert was arrested for drunk and disorderly conduct."

When Britney had shown up at her office this morning, Lauren's schedule had already been packed. However, she'd agreed to see Britney and accompany her to court when the desperate young woman had said Greg had sent her. Apparently, the director of the women's shelter had called Greg to fix the damaged front door, and Greg had, in turn, recommended to Britney that she come see Lauren for help.

Britney frowned at her, hissing, "You make it sound so bad."

Lauren ignored her. "Mr. Colbert shouted threats of physical violence against his wife as the police hauled him away. Mrs. Colbert didn't tell me that, Your Honor, but I read it on the report I obtained from the police this morning."

Judge Brooks nailed Britney with hard stare. "Is this true?"

Finally, the woman's cool reserve cracked and tears filled her eyes. "Yeah. Yeah, it's all true. I'm scared. I love Bub. But I'm afraid he might hurt me. He just needs to get through this binge, Judge. Once he does, everything will go back to normal."

Normal. What was that, anyway? Lauren wondered. Her 'normal' had certainly shifted and changed over time.

Before trouble had trounced on her and Greg, their normal had been pretty magnificent. Yes, he'd been busy running his business and she running hers, but when they came together, he'd filled her life chock-full of spontaneous fun and excitement.

Once they'd split, her 'normal' had become nothing but work; clients, lawsuits, court appearances. Not that that was a bad thing, she mused. She enjoyed her job. But playfulness, silly acts of frivolous amusement—something that had never come naturally to her—had become non-existent the day she'd asked Greg for a divorce.

Now that she was dating Scott, 'normal' had once again changed, but rather than the routine becoming livelier, as a woman would naturally expect when she had a new man in her life, it had remained mainly monotonous. Scott's modus operandi was, unfortunately, predictable. The long hours they worked usually necessitated their meeting at some restaurant or other, and as they ate, they discussed their workdays. Her clients' legal dilemmas, which she found fascinating, made his eyes glaze over, and she was bored rigid hearing his insurance tales.

Once they'd gone to a movie after dinner, and Lauren had decided there was nothing more tiresome than the ho-hum dinner-and-a-movie date. They'd sat next to each other in the dark, not touching, not talking, not even sharing popcorn since they'd just eaten. She wanted to get to know this man, wanted him to get to know her, but for some reason that didn't seem to be happening.

She and Greg had rarely gone to a cinema center. Most of the movies they watched had been streamed. Watching from the comfort of their own sofa afforded a much cozier, private setting in which to enjoy their favorite genres... everything from psychological thrillers to romantic comedies. Greg would call her out of the blue and whisper, "Naked movie night?" and she would spend the rest of the day anticipating all the sexy excitement promised in the short question. A smile pulled at her lips until she remembered where she was, what she was doing.

She missed the 'normal' that Greg had brought to her life. The realization made her muscles go slack and the ink pen slipped from her fingers, clattering to the floor. She bent down to retrieve it, her head going woozy with the sudden insight. Her legs felt suddenly weak when she rose up, and the luxury of a chair being impossible at the moment, she locked her knees in place and clutched the legal pad to her chest.

Okay, so her ex had brought a great deal of exhilaration and fun into her life. He'd also brought plenty of heartache. Not on the same scale that Bubby Colbert brought to poor Britney's, but still...

Scott might not be the most exciting man to come down the pike. But he was ambitious and successful. He wasn't the kind of man who needed to be bailed out of trouble. At least, she didn't think he was. And she might not ever find out exactly who he was if she couldn't get the man to talk about something other than his job.

The sound of the gavel startled her.

"Counselor, the Temporary Protective Order is granted," Judge Brooks said. "Robert Walter Colbert is hereby ordered not to abuse, threaten to abuse, contact, attempt to contact or harass Britney Renee Colbert. He is to remain away from her place of employment and/or residence for the next thirty days. Mrs. Colbert, I hope you use this time to make some serious decisions about your situation."

"I will," Britney promised, wiping the tears from her eyes.

"Thank you, Judge." Lauren turned to collect her things.

Britney hovered near the defendant's table, brushing at her bangs and pulling at one sleeve, then the other, to cover the bruises on her wrists. Her gaze hopped from Lauren to the double doors to some other part of the courtroom and back again as if she wasn't sure what to do or where to go. "Guess that solves my problem." She shrugged. "At least for the next month."

"I'll see that your husband is served with a copy of the order. If you need me, you've got my number." Lauren snapped her briefcase shut, silently wishing every woman's 'man troubles' could be so easily solved.

* * *

The autumn breeze that cooled the evening air that very same evening did little to temper Lauren's heated skin or the need thrumming through her body. Scott broke off the sultry kiss, his breathing as labored as hers.

"You're killin' me," he whispered, his voice rusty.

"I'm killing you?" She could barely get the words out.

Lauren had endured yet another dinner at yet

another restaurant where conversation had been sparse and unproductive. She knew little more about him now than she had when they'd arrived. Sure, she could give up. She could tell Scott she wasn't interested in seeing him any more, that they had little in common and that she didn't see the relationship going anywhere. But Lauren firmly believed they did have at least one commonality.

They both enjoyed kissing.

And, good mercy, Ms. Percy, the man was an extraordinary kisser!

"You want to go to my place?" he asked her. "I could... ah, put on some music, and... and... um, open a bottle of wine."

Clearly, his true desire (which she was absolutely positive matched her own)—that they tear off each other's clothes and race for the bed—was making it difficult for him to think of any other activities to suggest.

"That sounds wonderful." Her breathing was still thick as she lifted her chin so he could nibble on her neck a moment longer.

He pulled back and looked at her, hunger raging in his heavy-lidded blue gaze. "Follow me." He swallowed and tried to smile. "We'll be there in twenty minutes, tops."

Not more than half an hour later, the soft strains of a woodwinds concerto drifted on the air, glasses of deep red merlot sat untouched on the coffee table and Lauren and Scott were once again muzzling, having foregone even the house tour in order to get right to the business of enjoying the comfort of the couch.

Scott cradled the back of her neck with one hand while his other roved slowly and freely over her body; cupping her breast, sliding over her waist and hip, massaging her thigh. Lauren was certain he meant to tease her to the point of insanity.

Come on, come on, she wanted to urge. Let's get naked. Now!

She'd spied the budge in his trousers, knew he wanted the same thing she did. Still, the seconds ticked by, she'd given him every sign she could think of, yet he seemed perfectly content to kiss her and touch her—with way too much fabric between them.

What were they? Eighth graders?

Granted, she hadn't dated in a lot of years. What did she know? Maybe this was the 'in' thing. Maybe couples didn't go all the way anymore. Maybe they simply kissed and teased each other until they went stark raving mad.

What a load of bull! Of course, couples did it. Human behavior couldn't have changed that much in seventeen years, for cryin' out loud. What was wrong with this man?

The question should have waved red flags in her brain, but she was too pre-occupied at the moment to pay attention. Her nipples were puckered tight enough to give her a headache, her pulse throbbed hot and heavy in her deepest, naughtiest places, and the only way to inhale much-needed oxygen was to drag it onto her lungs. Finally she could take it no longer.

"Scott—" her voice sounded strained even to her own ears as she freed two buttons of his shirt "—let's go to your bedroom."

He pulled back, and something that looked suspiciously like trepidation flashed in his eyes. Later, Lauren would realize that that, too, should have been a warning sign to be heeded.

"You want some sex?" he asked, eager as an energetic puppy.

The peculiar phrasing of his question made her grin. He spoke as if sex were something he carried around in his pocket, something to be doled out like breath mints or sticks of chewing gum.

"Yeah," she told him, her chuckle throaty and

sensual. "Actually, I do. I really, really do." Earlier she'd tossed her purse onto the floor next to the leg of the end table and she bent to reach for it. "I even came prepared."

Buying condoms wasn't something she'd ever done before. During her married life, Greg had taken care of that chore when she hadn't been taking the pill. And for the thirteen months she'd been separated—and completely celibate—there had been no need for birth control of any kind. But Norma Jean had pointed out her Big O problem last month, and then she'd started playing suck face with Scott so she'd decided she'd better get her butt to the pharmacy to buy a box of Trojans.

She'd quickly discovered that the prophylactic counter offered a variety of overwhelming choices. Lubricated. Non-lubricated. Smooth. Thin. Ribbed. Ultra ribbed. With and without spermicide. With and without 'tingling' lotion. She even found one with a vibrating ring attached, for goodness sake. Condom companies sure had made advances.

While she'd stood there pondering the pros and cons of each little package of worry-free pleasure, a lanky teen had approached and come to a halt beside her. He'd snatched a box from the shelf, then turned and looked at her. Then he'd offered her a knowing grin.

Twenty years ago, she might have felt embarrassed, but that day she'd experienced a surprising empowerment. She'd smiled back, and then nodded as if to say, "Yes, I'm doing it." The young man had chuckled before ambling down the aisle toward the cash register.

Lauren held up the square, gold-colored beauties for Scott.

His mouth cocked sexily and he said, "You did come prepared."

He plucked the two condoms from her fingers and then he stood, reaching out his hand. She slid her palm into it and he tugged her off the couch.

It was only after she crossed the threshold of his bedroom that she noticed things began to go awry. Masculine furniture with its straight lines and dark stain filled the spacious room. The thick, burgundy-colored spread that covered the king-sized bed looked inviting.

Scott let go of her hand and began to undress... *himself*. Several awkward seconds passed with her just standing there watching him. Then, not knowing what else to do, she slipped off her shoes.

The act of unzipping her skirt and unbuttoning

her blouse doused the fire that had been blazing inside her. Greg had always—

No. She shook her head, refusing to go there. This was neither the time nor the place for memories of sex with her ex.

Okay, so making love with Scott was going to be different. Different could be good. Different would be good. Different was what she really wanted, wasn't it?

She stripped down to her panties and bra, just one of several small, cute scraps of matching lace sets she'd bought and worn during her last couple of dates with Scott just in case an opportunity like this should arise.

He padded to the bed, completely naked, and threw back the coverlet and top sheet. He turned to her and circled his hands like someone exercising away a bout of carpal tunnel, the look on his face either anticipation or impatience, she couldn't tell which.

"Come on, come on," he encouraged.

Gut instinct told her he didn't appreciate in the least her sexy undies, that his words and hand gestures were signs that he wanted her nude. So she slipped out of her expensive underwear.

She stood next to him as he ripped open the

condom package. No touching. No whispering of endearments. No intimacy at all. The scene became a little too stark for her liking.

Once he'd successfully donned the single-digit latex glove, he held up the sheet for her to climb into bed. She eased onto the mattress, sliding her legs down between the cool, cotton sheets. If she could only get him to kiss her again; she was certain the sparks would fly once more.

Scott hopped into bed beside her. "Okay, let's get this party started."

Get the party started—all over again—is what they would have to do. She'd been oh-so-ready just a few minutes ago. She'd felt primed. Deliciously horny. Damp in her nether regions even. But the strange disconnect between their passionate foreplay on the couch and the 'undressing phase' had completely knocked her off kilter.

She stroked his chest, determined to get back into the groove. "Kiss me."

"All right," he groaned.

He rolled toward her... and things suddenly turned oddly surreal.

Lauren realized she'd lost her groove, totally and completely. She tried to find it—she closed her eyes, focused—but the harder she tried to concentrate on the moment, the more bizarre the circumstance became. All too quickly, he went still.

"Man, oh, man, that was good," he said, sliding into the spot next to her and placing a perfunctory kiss on her jaw. "That was so good."

Sweat had turned his brow slick and glossy. He heaved a deep sigh, gave his pillow a thump and closed his eyes.

She blinked in the dim light, and then she whispered his name.

"Mmmm?" But his breathing was even and easy.

If Lauren's mind hadn't been spinning in such a state of confusion, she'd have laughed at the utter ridiculousness of the situation. She'd been the one to suggest they have sex. She'd been the one who had come prepared with lacy undies and ribbed condoms. For her pleasure. (Yeah, right.) She'd been the one in desperate need of a Big O.

Oh, yes, if she could collect herself and think straight, she would see the hilarity of it all. But as it was, she merely stared up at the ceiling, feeling hollow and unsatisfied, as she wondered what in the world had just happened.

Chapter Fourteen

There are worst things than bad sex...right?

~Lauren Flynn

"**W**rong." Norma Jean chuckled. "But judging from the pitiful look on your face, Lauren, you really do want to believe that." She dunked her tea bag into a mug of hot water. "Well, I'm your friend, woman. And I know you wouldn't want me to tell you anything but the cold, hard truth. There is absolutely nothing worse than bad sex."

Lauren grimaced. She'd been afraid that's what she was going to hear.

Her sexual fiasco with Scott had upset her so badly that she'd come into the office and spilled her guts. She'd told Norma Jean everything, from the monotonous dinner dates to the toe-curling good-night kisses. Recounting her fleeting and ineffectual bedroom romp had tightened a fist-sized knot in her stomach.

"Well, you know," Lauren confessed, "maybe it was partly my fault. You and I both know I'm, you know... having that 'O' problem. I've definitely let things go too long."

"I'll say." Norma snickered.

Ignoring her, Lauren squirted honey onto her teaspoon and stirred it into her tea. "I was strung tighter than a guitar string, Norma Jean. Maybe I was so desperate that my body just—" she shrugged "—shut down."

Norma just shook her head. "Don't you dare take the blame for this. Let me remind you of the description you gave not two minutes ago." She ticked off the first item with a lift of her thumb. "You said the moment you walked into his bedroom it was every man for himself."

Lauren cringed. Yep, she'd said that.

"You said," Norma continued, straightening her index finger, "it was if you'd taken your car in for a complete overhaul and all you got was your oil checked."

The knot in her stomach tightened. Yep, she'd said that, too.

"You said—" Norma Jean's brown eyes flashed with indignation "—it took more time for you to blink twice than it had for him to get his rocks off... and then the selfish son of bitch fell asleep before you could say goodnight Irene." She lost count as she held up both hands, fingers splayed wide.

Steam rose from Lauren's mug when she picked it up. "Now, now," she chided softly. "I never called him names. And I don't know any Irene." She blew across the surface of her tea before taking a tentative sip. "I read somewhere that sex can have that affect on some men. They become so relaxed, they just fall asleep."

Norma shook her head again, her shoulders rounding. Apparently, her angry storm had blown itself out.

"I can't believe you're trying to find excuses for this creep. Or that you're willing to somehow make this your fault. The way you described how you gathered up your clothes and skulked out of there so you wouldn't have to face him makes it sound like you feel guilty."

Lauren couldn't deny the truth. She had felt guilty. She'd dressed as if the house had been ablaze, and she'd driven away feeling completely confused. Should she feel angry that he'd seemed to forget all about her, or should she be embarrassed because she'd somehow dropped out of the game?

Even though she had made all those complaints to Norma about her disappointing sexual experience, Lauren still couldn't get it out of her head that Scott seemed the right man for her.

"He really isn't a creep." She strived to keep the whine out of her tone, but knew she failed.

"Uh-huh, right. He isn't a creep. He's just a selfish jerk who engages in lopsided love making."

The terminology was too fitting not to be appreciated, and here Lauren had thought her overshadowing gloom would keep her from finding anything funny in this conversation. Once she got her mirth under control and she'd wrestled down her grin, she stressed, "He really is a nice guy, Norma Jean."

Picking up her mug once again, Norma muttered, "Outside of the bedroom, maybe." She rested her hip against the edge of the counter. "Please tell me you plan to forget about him, Lauren. If you try to ignore his obvious lack of prowess, you're in for nothing but unhappy frustration. There are tons of fish in the sea, hon. Do yourself a favor and recast your line."

Lauren absently picked up a vanilla wafer from the basket and took a bite. The crisp cookie was sweet on her tongue.

Maybe Norma Jean was right. Maybe she should just give up the idea of going out with Scott. But maybe she could salvage this. Maybe she could talk to him. Maybe she could make him understand that she needed a little more attention, or rather some attention—

"Oh, hell," Norma said in obvious disgust. "I can see that brain of yours churning. There are wisps of smoke coming out of your ears. You're still trying to figure out how to make it work, aren't you?"

Lauren sighed guiltily, popping the rest of the cookie into her mouth and brushing the crumbs from her fingers.

"Honey, I can't stress enough how important good sex is in a healthy relationship. Couples need to be compatible. They need to pay close attention to each other's needs. They have to feel comfortable enough to enjoy each other. There can't be any self-consciousness in the bedroom, Lauren. There has to be lots of give and take. Lots."

Something about Norma Jean changed during this short lecture. Lauren couldn't say if it was the animation in her voice or her facial expression or her body language, but something made Lauren's attention perk.

She studied her friend, noting the devilishness that sparkled in her brown gaze. Suddenly, Lauren felt squeamish. "Oh, no," she breathed. "Don't tell me."

Norma's grin inched from ear to ear. "Oh, yeah. You got it." She waggled her fingers over her head and performed a happy little shimmy of her fanny.

Lauren took a small backward step. "But you two haven't been seeing each other that long."

"Longer than you and your Rapid Ralphie."

Lauren was too bowled over to even think about taking up for Scott. "But my dad is a gentleman."

Heat flushed Norma Jean's cheeks. "Oh, I totally agree. He is. A very conscientious gentleman, I might add. He did things to me that I've never—"

"Norma! TMI! TMI!" Lauren slammed down her mug, plainly seeing a good portion of the contents slosh over the rim but caring only about running away as fast as her feet could carry her. She rushed from the break room, Norma's delighted laughter ringing in her ears.

"Come on, Lauren," she called after her. "Old farts gotta have fun, too."

Making a bee-line for her office, Lauren snatched up her jacket and purse and then headed back into the reception area.

"I've got to make a quick run to the barn," she told Norma Jean who now stood in the threshold of the break room, leaning casually on the jamb. Lauren tried to ignore the utter delight turning Norma's face to a beautiful and amazing work of art. No doubt about it, the woman looked euphoric.

"Another one of the carousel horses is finished," she explained, her hand bracing open the front door. "I have to meet Howard and give him a check."

Without waiting for a reply, she stalked out into the bright sunshine.

Had Norma Jean actually described what she was doing with grumpy Lew Hunkavic as fun? Lauren shivered, slipping into her car and shoving the key into the ignition.

As the engine revved to life, she was hit with a realization that forced a loud, incredulous groan from her throat. She closed her eyes and rested her forehead on the steering wheel.

For the love of Pete, her seventy-year-old father was having better sex than she was. Life just wasn't fair.

Chapter Fifteen

The first thing I do in the morning
is brush my teeth and sharpen my tongue.
~Dorothy Parker

"**O**n a rare Friday afternoon, Lauren had found herself with no client appointments and no court appearances scheduled. She'd told Norma Jean to turn on the answering machine and take the afternoon off, then she'd high-tailed it to the library, checked out half a dozen or so books and was now seated on a makeshift chair made of a rickety wooden sawhorse while she poured over information on merry-go-rounds, a chilled bottle of peach-flavored green tea at her elbow and the silence and seclusion of the barn wrapping her in a restful cocoon. She hadn't felt this relaxed in ages.

Sure she had work needing to be done, clients with upcoming court dates, briefs to write, case law to research, but in her line of work those things would never go away completely. Add to that the fact that she still had to figure out what she was going to do about Scott. He'd called her cell and left a voice message, and he'd called the office, too, Norma had told her. Lauren wasn't sure what to say to him; all she knew for certain was that she didn't want a repeat of those awful three minutes they'd spent together in his bed.

However, even though she had unfinished business in both her professional and her personal life, she was in dire need of a break. A break from the office and a break from worrying about her miserable sex life.

While trolling the internet investigating prices and the best way to sell the carousel animals, she'd seen many a warning to buyers against being deceived and purchasing a figure that wasn't authentic. It had made her curious enough to want check to see what, exactly, made a merry-go-round animal 'genuine' rather than 'fake.'

Authentic carousel animals, she read, were

never carved from a solid block of wood. The carver began with a hollow box that reduced the figure's weight and allowed for normal expansion and contraction of the wood and prevented excess cracking. Lauren knew her animals were hollow. The painter she'd hired, Howard Largent, had told her so. He'd disassembled one of them each week from its metal couplings and carried it to his truck, unaided.

The hum of an engine outside drew her attention away from the books she'd spread open on the workbench. The motor went silent, and by the time she heard the vehicle door slam shut, Lauren was halfway to the door. She'd been certain Scott, Jr. had classes and had hoped to have the barn and the whole afternoon to herself.

The wide plank door wobbled on its hinges when she pushed it open. Seeing Greg sauntering across the grassy expanse sent a thrill shooting through her. The reaction was unexpected. Visceral. Uncontrollable.

She let her gaze dart off to the horizon behind him, pressing cool fingers to her suddenly warm cheek. She jerked her hand from her face, collecting herself with a deep breath.

"Hey, there." Greg lifted his hand and then let

it fall to his side. "I stopped in and had lunch with Lew today and he told me you'd be out here."

Lauren kept her smile cool. "I haven't had an afternoon off in awhile."

He stopped a few feet from her. "I called your cell to see if you were busy," he told her. "But it went right to voice mail."

"I turned it off. I needed a little peace and quiet."

Greg nodded. His dark eyes darted from her face to her feet to the inner recesses of the barn.

"If you're busy, I can, ah... go. I don't want to bother you."

"No," she said, her backward step an unspoken invitation inside. "I've got the heater running. Thanks for leaving it behind. I was just doing a little reading." She walked toward the workbench and the books scattered across its surface. "Did you know that European merry-go-rounds turn in a clockwise direction while American-made ones turn counter-clockwise?" She reached the bench and turned to face him. Without waiting for him to respond, she explained further. "Apparently, European craftsmen were focused on mounting the horse properly, so the left flank faces outward." She chuckled as she added, "And in famous American prize-winning tradition, we changed the direction in order to capture the brass ring. Most people are right handed."

His black eyes shined like polished stones as he studied her face intently. Finally, he said, "I haven't seen you smile in a long time."

The curl at the corners of her mouth slipped and suddenly she felt self-conscious. "So—" she shoved her hands into the pockets of her cable knit cardigan "—how are you? I haven't seen you for, what? A month?" Since that embarrassing episode on the merry-go-round when she'd nearly lost control. "You doing okay?"

"Yeah." He nodded, sliding his hands into his back pockets. "I'm doing just fine," he told her. "How about you? You look good, Lauren. You look really good."

His compliment made her blush. She dipped her chin in an attempt to hide the unsettling reaction and snuggled her hands deeper into her pockets.

"Lew told me you're seeing someone."

She nearly gave herself whiplash jerking her gaze up to meet his. A frown bit deeply into her brow. It was difficult to tell if the concern on his face was caused by the news he'd learned or by her reaction to his comment.

"Is that why you're here? The two of you shouldn't be discussing my—"

"No, no. Hold on." He lifted up both hands, palms out. "Lauren, no names were mentioned. No details were discussed. You're free to do what you want. I was just... making small talk."

His choice of words was an abrupt reminder of the difficulty she and Scott had, time and again, simply trying to get to know each other. While they'd been together, she and Greg had often debated topics for long stretches of time. Communication had never been a problem between them. Not until the end, anyway.

As if he'd crawled right into her head and read her thoughts, he said, "I hate walking on eggshells. We used to be able to talk about anything, Lauren. Even if we held opposing views, we could talk about something all day long and not argue. Now all we seem to do when we see each other is fight."

Thankfully, he didn't mention their last meeting here at the barn.

Frustration tightened his handsome face. He was right. And it wasn't him. It was her. These days, when it came to Greg, she was always ready for an argument. Even though she'd tried to come to terms with what had happened between them, it seemed that remnants of anger continued to simmer. But she honestly wanted to let it all go. The tension in her neck and shoulders relaxed when she sighed.

"I am seeing the father of one my clients," she said. "His name's Scott Shaw. We've been out—" a weird sensation swirled in her chest, forcing her gaze to shift from his "—I don't know, a few times."

Why was it so hard to get that out? She and Greg were divorced; she owed him no allegiance. Yet the idea of him discovering that she'd slept with Scott made her outright panicky. Maybe it wasn't so much him finding out she'd gone to bed with another man as much as it was that she didn't want him knowing the experience had been such an utter nightmare.

He looked a little confused. "Your dad said he thought things were getting serious. That you were having dinner with his guy several times a week."

"Why are you so interested?" she asked, pleasantly surprised that she was able to keep her tone light and cordial. "I'm dating... so what? You're dating, too. We should be happy for each other."

His frown went full-throttle. "I don't know what you're talking about."

"Oh, come on, Greg." She pulled her hands free of her pockets and let them fall easily to her sides. "Jo Leigh didn't tell you we met at the courthouse? She said you and she were dating." She shrugged. "Well, she asked me if I minded if you and she dated, and I told her you were free to do as you chose."

He shook his head, seemingly confounded. "She's invited me to eat dinner with her and Tracy a couple of times." He cocked his head, shrugging a muscular shoulder. "But that was only because I was working late on her remodel. She wants the garage finished before the end of the month so she can open the daycare. I've been working like a madman to get the job done."

Lauren listened as he made light of his relationship with Jo Leigh and then veered the topic in another direction. Clearly, neither of them was comfortable talking about their personal lives.

"I'll bet you're good with Tracy," she said softly.

He smiled. "She's a great kid." He turned so he could lean his hip against the workbench. "She comes out to the garage every day after school to help me." He chuckled. "Gets underfoot is mostly what she does, but I keep her hopping and fetching for me."

The warmth in his voice when he spoke of Jo Leigh's daughter stirred up an odd remorse.

"Are you ever sorry?" She sat down on the sawhorse. "That we never had kids, I mean."

He crossed his arms over his chest. "I don't like to waste time with regrets."

She did know that about him. "But you don't ever think about it? Don't you ever wonder?"

Greg tilted his head a bit. "I didn't use to. But spending time with Tracy has really been... enlightening. Kids have a way of brightening up the day. They're fun. And open. And honest." He went quiet. "I think having a baby would have changed our lives."

Lauren wondered if a child might have tempered her personality a little. Made her less intense about her career, her aspirations... her life in general. Becoming a parent most certainly would have opened her world to new experiences, and it also might have softened her heart. She sighed.

Then she remembered how hard it had been to lose her mother. How grief-stricken she'd been. How desolate and, yes, frightened and vulnerable she'd felt. Even though she'd had her father, losing her mother had been... indescribably difficult.

"Your mom dying when you were so young had an awful impact on you," Greg said. "I knew that."

She was once again struck with the uncanny notion that she and he had some sort of odd psychic connection that allowed him to so easily pick up on her thoughts. He understood her in a way no one else could.

He shifted his weight to one foot, resting one ankle on the other. "I'd hoped we'd eventually find the right time to have children. But when that didn't happen—" his mouth flattened for the briefest of moments "—well, it just didn't happen."

She swallowed. "And you never pushed me."

His shoulders lifted and then fell. "That wouldn't have been right. A baby is something that two people have to agree on."

Several long, silent seconds stretched out between them.

Finally, Lauren sighed. "You'd have been a wonderful father, Greg." She looked at the toes of her shoes. "I feel bad because—" she paused, unable to look him in the eyes "—well, because I can't help but think I made the decision for both of us. My career took—"

"Don't do that, Lauren. Don't beat yourself up."

His voice was soft. He didn't move, didn't reach

out to her or touch her, but he didn't have to. She still felt exceedingly comforted.

"What we had together was good," he told her firmly. "Yeah, the last months were a little rocky. But that was my fault. I take full responsibility. Despite the end, though, we had a lot of good years." After a beat, he asked, "Didn't we?"

She nodded. "Yeah. We did."

It actually felt good to talk to him without anger getting in the way. They shared a lot of history. A lot of good history. Small snatches of it had been coming to her in bits and pieces over the past few weeks.

Tucking her hands between her knees, she lifted her chin. "Why didn't you come to me, Greg?" Although it had never entered her head to ask the question before today, she knew down to the bone that she'd been desperate for an answer for a very long time. "If you'd have come to me sooner, we might have been able to save the store. I still can't believe that we lost your father's hardware store." There was no anger in the statement. Just a great deal of sadness. "How did it happen? Why didn't you say something before it was too late?"

His gaze slid from hers. "I don't know. Male pride, I guess. I didn't want you to know."

After a moment, she said, "You really didn't think I'd find out?" The grin in her voice drew his gaze to hers, but his expression remained somber.

He released a pent-up exhalation. "Things started going bad right after Dad died."

She was surprised to hear he'd had trouble that early. Daniel Flynn had passed away from complications of an undiagnosed heart defect. That had been seven years ago.

"Dad had let a lot of people run up a lot of bills," Greg told her. "Then two contractors defaulted on their accounts. One went bankrupt, the other left town in the dead of night. I tried to implement changes, but customers seemed to like the way Dad did business. He let them pay for supplies in installments, or sometimes not at all until they were paid for their jobs. But it was an old-fashioned system that slowly but surely fell apart. Before I knew it, I was up to my eyeballs in debt. I tried to fix things. Tried to force people to pay what they owed. Refused to run tabs." He shook his head. "And then that big home improvement store was built outside of town, and that was all she wrote."

Lauren took a moment simply to look at him. She'd forgotten how his eyes would crinkle and his mouth would quirk up when he relayed a funny story. Or how his dark gaze could turn intense while he was listening attentively to something she had to say or when he was telling her something drop-dead serious. She saw that same concentration in his onyx eyes right now.

She'd missed this, she thought out of the blue. She missed him. And how they used to talk about... everything. Even when they'd fussed, as couples often do, they had always found a way to work things out. When had that changed for them?

Suddenly, she ached with missing him. Him and all the good things he'd brought into her life.

A frown bit into her brow, and something dark and heavy descended on her. The urge to cry welled up, taunting her fiercely. Her eyelids burned, and as she fought back tears, she immediately recognized what was beleaguering her. She swallowed in an attempt to loosen the unyielding knot of grief that had formed in her throat. She'd been so busy feeling hurt and angry about how their lives had spun out of control that she hadn't had the opportunity to mourn all that they had lost.

Looking off toward the merry-go-round, Lauren

inhaled a slow, calming breath. The last thing she wanted was to lose control of her emotions over something that neither of them could do a thing about. What was done was done.

Silence pulled, thinner and tighter, with each passing second.

Greg must have followed her gaze. "Wow," he breathed. He pushed himself away from the workbench and walked across the barn floor. "Howie's doing a great job."

Relief washed through her. She needed to have something—anything—else to focus on beside the horrible heaviness pressing on her chest. Greg, too, must have been looking for a way out of the chilly shadows of the past that they had inadvertently allowed to close around them.

"They look brand new, don't you think?" The dry, corroded sound of her voice was fairly easy to ignore.

Greg glided gentle fingertips over the zebra's glossy paint, down the figure's thick neck, over its back, and Lauren couldn't help but remember that there'd been a time when he'd touched her with the same gentleness. She closed her eyes, the clear-as-crystal memory churning in her mind.

When she looked across the barn, he was still

admiring the zebra. The glossy black and white stripes stood out in vivid contrast.

"I never even noticed before," he commented. "They have glass eyes." He must have spied the other refurbished figures. "They're beautiful."

One Arabian had been given a white pearlescent coat; while another stallion looked its complete opposite in gleaming ebony paint. Howard had done an extraordinary job on the animals' trappings, as well; saddles, blankets, fringed breast bands, scarf draping, tassels—all sported bold carnival colors.

He turned toward her, but Lauren's gaze was riveted to his hands where they remained stretched out on the zebra's back. The pulse in her neck throbbed.

Pulling himself up onto the platform, he went to give the black stallion a closer examination, and she was grateful for the opportunity to quiet her erratic heartbeat.

"Did you see this? This horse has actual expression in his face, Lauren. It looks fierce. And this one—" he moved to the Arabian "—looks gentle as a lamb."

The awe in Greg's voice was mesmerizing, but Lauren forced herself to stay put on the crossbar of the sawhorse. When he became excited about something, his enthusiasm quickly turned infectious and getting caught up in it probably wouldn't be wise. Not unless she wanted a repeat of the last time they'd been on the merry-go-round together.

She still hadn't told Greg her intentions to sell the figures. Once he found out she meant to dismantle the carousel, she suspected he wouldn't be happy. She'd have to tell him eventually. Sooner rather than later, she guessed, seeing that Howard was finishing the animals quicker than she'd expected. They couldn't be sold without bases, and for that, she'd need Greg's expert opinion... and probably his carpentry skills. If he'd agree to offer them.

The best thing to do would be to just tell him. Get it over with. Like ripping away a band-aid from newly healed skin. Worrying about it only made the ordeal worse later on.

Instead, she said, "Your friend Howard is a talented artist."

"He give you a good price?"

She nodded even though his attention was elsewhere. "He did. Thanks for calling in your chips."

He stepped off the platform and approached her. "Speaking of money," he murmured, reaching for his back pocket. "I brought you something."

"What's this?" she asked, accepting the white business-sized envelope that had been folded in half.

"I was going to leave it at the house this afternoon." He took a small backward step. "But Lew talked me into bringing it here."

Although he was doing his best to hide it, she sensed a slight and sudden edginess in his tone that made her uneasy. She made no move to open it. "What is it, Greg?"

He offered her a small, hesitant smile. "A cashier's check."

"What? But why? For what?" As the short questions shot from her mouth like bullets, she lifted the flap and pulled out the check. All those zeros made her gasp.

Then she frowned at the check and finally at him. "Where did you get forty thousand dollars?"

Rather than answer her question, he said, "I know this doesn't cover everything. But it's a solid start. You can deposit it in your retirement fund. Or you can use some of it to set up your dad in his own place again." He inched toward her. "I'd have had more, but you forced me out of the barn. I needed a security deposit on the apartment. And rent. And utilities." He rubbed his palms up and down his thighs. "The bills never seem to let up. I'll give you the rest just as soon as—"

"Wait, Greg. Stop." She took another look at the check, squinting at the number typed in the amount box. She didn't know if she'd expected it to change, or what, but it hadn't. "What is this? Where did you get this kind of money? What are you doing? You don't owe me anything. Didn't you hear a word I said in court that day? Judge Brooks told you... " Then the meaning behind the words Greg had just spoken slowly seeped into her brain and her voice trailed, her gaze finding and then searching his for several long seconds.

Realization made her mouth go dry and her head cock to one side. "You were living in this barn so you could save money? To pay me back?"

The pauses she inadvertently placed between each question made her sound slow-witted. Hell, that's pretty much how she felt right now as she tried to figure out why he would do this.

He, on the other hand, expressed a clear and open uncertainty, in his countenance and in his body language, as if he couldn't decide whether answering her questions would turn out to be a good thing or land him in more trouble. Finally, he answered with two short, jerky nods before going still, obviously waiting, bracing himself even, for her reaction.

Lauren felt as if she were moving in low gear, thinking in slow motion. This didn't make sense. There simply wasn't another human on earth who could unsettle her more than Greg Flynn.

"I don't understand." She stood, the check in one hand, the creased envelope in the other. "You don't owe me any money. Greg, the law clearly states—"

"I know what the law says," he told her calmly. "I know what you said. I know what the judge said. I know I'm not legally bound to anything, Lauren. But I am—" his gaze darted toward the ceiling as he evidently searched for word "—honor bound. I cost you, Lauren. I cost you, big time. I intend to make it up to you."

"What?" she asked, continuing to shake her head. "Are you buying back the land? The barn and the merry-go-round?"

"No. No. This is yours. The judge gave it to you. I have no qualms with that. In fact, I want you to have it, Lauren. I want you to have it all. To make up for everything that happened. Everything I put you through."

He was saying all the right words. They should have been the right words, anyway, she thought. But apparently they weren't. Because... apparently... they were grating on her.

"Do you know what this place is worth?" she asked him quietly.

The question took him aback. "Worth? Not a whole lot. At the moment. But Sterling is growing. And before too long, people are going to be looking for land to build on. The land's worth holding on to."

"And you're willing to just give it away?" She lifted her shoulders, her arms, her hands. "Just like that? You're willing to give up your land, your money, your time and talent. You're willing to give everything away, aren't you, Greg?" She looked at him, shaking her head. "You're no longer just making poor business decisions. You've now moved into the realm of sheer stupidity."

His brows rose and his lips parted, but no sound came out. He raked his fingers though his hair. "Lauren, I don't know what you're talking about."

"You've given your land to me." She placed her palm on her chest.

"The judge did that."

"But you just said you have no qualms about it," she accused. "You've given your money—" she shook the check at him "—to me. You've given your time and talent, free of charge, to Jo Leigh. Keep this up and you won't have a pot to pee in."

"What are you talking about?" He looked at her as though he thought she'd lost her mind. "Yes, I gave you money. Only because I owe it." He frowned. "But I didn't give anything to Jo Leigh."

"That's not true. You know it and I know it."

Once again, she'd stunned him into silence. He looked completely aghast. But slowly his expression tightened with ruddy ire.

"So I'm not just stupid," he said, his tone dangerously low, "I'm a stupid liar. Tell me, Lauren, do you ever cut your gums on that sharp tongue of yours?"

In all the years she'd known him, she could probably count on one hand the number of times she'd seen Greg angry. He was an easy-going man who didn't lose his temper. Lauren pulled herself up straighter and met his glare. Maybe this was a good thing, she decided. Maybe she could shock him into watching out for his own best interests.

"You need to take this check back, Greg," she

said, amazed by the composure with which she spoke. "And you need to stop working for free."

"You're keeping that check." His eyes narrowed. "And I have been paid for every minute I've worked for Jo Leigh Stapleton."

Lauren wanted to march up to him and stuff that expensive slip of paper into his shirt pocket. She wanted to force him to take the good advice she was offering. Instead, she asked, "If that's true, then why would she tell me you're working for free?"

His gaze never wavered from hers. "Are you sure that's what she said? Think, Lauren. Think hard. Because I seriously doubt that Jo Leigh would tell you something that wasn't true. She's not that kind of person."

How dare he insinuate that she had heard Jo Leigh wrong?

"I'm positive that's what she said. She told me you were converting her garage. 'I'm getting it all for free' were her exact words."

Greg's jaw muscle ticked. "You're bound and determined to criticize and condemn every thing I do, aren't you?" He tucked a fisted hand on his hip. "I mess up once, and now I can't do anything right. How could I have saved forty thousand dollars to give to you in just a year's time if I wasn't getting paid for the work I'm doing? Did it ever occur to you that she might have gotten the money from someplace? Because that's what she did. She applied for a government grant. Especially for single mothers. To start a new business."

A light-headed feeling came over Lauren. It was as if she were filled with helium and Greg had poked her with a sharp needle that had caused a slow leak. Her righteous anger lazily deflated. So did her haughty attitude.

She tried to swallow, but her mouth and throat had gone so dry the attempt was painful.

"I thought I could somehow say or do something to make everything up to you," he said, his gaze set on something high on the plank wall behind her. "To fix my mistake. To make it right. To assuage your anger so we could at least be civil to one another. But I can see now that won't ever be possible." His black eyes found hers and he glared for a long, drawn-out moment. "I can also see you're not the same woman I once knew."

He looked at her for a second or two longer, and then he stalked away without another word.

She stood there with her heart in her throat, a voice in her head screaming out for her to do something, say something. She should apologize. She should at least give him his money. Taking it wouldn't be right. But she figured she'd done enough damage for one day. So she continued to stand there, listening as the barn door tapped shut, as his truck engine revved and then settled into a hum before fading away as he drove off the property and down Skeeter Neck Road.

Chapter Sixteen

Health nuts are going to feel stupid some day,
lying in hospitals, dying of nothing.
~Red Foxx

Lauren opened her eyes, instantly wide awake. Moonlight cast a silvery glimmer across her bedroom, pulling long shadows from the dresser, chest of drawers and chair. She sat up and looked around the room, alert and listening for whatever it was that had snatched her from sleep.

A barely audible hum droned from somewhere in the darkness. After listening closer, she was able to make out what sounded like a murmuring voice.

She tossed back the blanket and sheet, glancing at the bedside clock to see the green glow of 3:04.

Her robe and slippers were nearby, and she slipped into both before heading to the bedroom door.

Once she'd stepped out into the upstairs hallway, she realized that the low mumbling was the sound of a television infomercial. Her dad must still be awake, or he'd fallen asleep and left the TV on.

When she had arrived home from the barn, she'd found a note from him saying that he and Norma Jean were going out to dinner and that she shouldn't wait up for him. He'd been like a changed man since Norma had entered his life. Less grumpy. And there'd been fewer complaints. It had almost become a pleasure to share the house with him. Almost.

The small smile whisking across Lauren's mouth faded when she remembered feeling relieved that he'd been out. The incident at the barn had left her feeling guilty and upset, and she knew her father would have picked up on her unsettled state.

She'd showered and changed, had tried to eat. Finally, she'd taken a few briefs to her room and climbed into bed with them and a cup of steaming chamomile tea. Her dad still hadn't come home by the time she'd started yawing and snapped off her light.

The oak banister was cool against her fingers as she descended the stairs.

Do you ever cut your gums on that sharp tongue of yours?

Greg's angry question reverberated in her head, and as it did, guilt gathered like a fist in the pit of her belly. Arrogance was such an ugly, offensive trait. She had always thought of herself as a confident person, but she never in her life would have believed she could be labeled as egotistical or presumptuous or contemptuous. Yet, she'd been all of those things and more when she'd talked to Greg this afternoon—no, when she'd talked at him. Yammered at him, really.

Then she thought back on the high-handed, holier-than-thou lecture she'd given him, a lecture she'd actually identified in her own mind as good advice. She shook her head, utterly nauseated by her behavior. She'd taken one snippet from her conversation with Jo Leigh and twisted it into a tangled mess. Her eagerness to see Greg as irresponsible and careless and, yes, even foolish, had completely blinded her to the fact that she just might be misconstruing Jo Leigh's comment.

From the base of the stairs, Lauren could see her father's sock-covered feet propped up on the raised base of his recliner. The television announcer urged his viewers to call the eight hundred number within the next ten minutes or risk losing the opportunity to own The Incredible Shed Stopper for the family dog or cat.

She entered the living room, and one look at her father's anguished expression had her rushing to his side.

"Dad? What's wrong? Where are you hurting?" The fact that he was in pain was clear. Sweat beaded his upper lip and forehead. His face and neck were pasty, his chest heaving with short, labored breaths.

"Heart's pounding," he finally ground out. He grimaced then, pressing a palm to his chest as if trying to scrub away the pain. "Hurts like the dickens."

"Don't move," she ordered. "I'll call for help."

Lauren raced to the kitchen, only to find the base of the remote telephone empty. She scanned the countertops and table, and then rushed into the dining room to check there. Snatching the phone off the table, she punched in the emergency number with trembling fingers. The operator's composed voice did nothing to calm her.

"Yes, this is an emergency; I need an

ambulance," she barked, stringing the sentences together. "My father's having a heart attack."

She reeled off her address as she made her way back toward the living room. A second, more powerful, dose of adrenalin shot through her when she saw her dad's eyes were closed.

"Dad?"

His skin felt clammy to the touch when she curled her fingers around his wrist to search for a pulse. The beat was thready and swift. His eyelids fluttered open, and fear clouded his hazel eyes. Lew Hunkavic had never been afraid of anything; the tension on his stark face made her feel helpless, and more frightened than she'd ever felt in her life.

"Ma'am? Hello?"

The voice in Lauren's ear startled her. She'd forgotten the telephone receiver she clutched in her hand like a lifeline.

"Is your father conscious?" the woman asked.

"Yes, yes." Lauren took hold of her dad's hand.

"Is he breathing?"

"Yes. But he's breathing really fast. Panting almost."

"Try to get him to calm down. Assure him that paramedics are on the way," the woman instructed. "I estimate their arrival time to be less than three minutes. I want you to stay on the line with me until they arrive."

Those three minutes turned out to be the longest of Lauren's life.

* * *

"You'll have to wait here," the nurse told her. "The doctor will come out and talk to you as soon as he can."

The nurse turned on one of her clunky, white Crocs and stalked back into the recesses of the ER, the heavy, double doors closing firmly behind her.

Sterling Memorial's waiting room was lit up as if it were noonday rather than the wee hours of the morning. Several people were scattered throughout the area, a couple of them obviously waiting to see a doctor. A television, mounted high on the wall, blared out international news, jarring her already frayed nerves. She found a seat as far from the noise as possible.

However, she was on her feet within seconds, pacing to the far end of the room and then back again.

The EMTs had bustled into the house, their prompt, efficient action lending Lauren a smidgen of relief that she and her father were no longer all alone in the crisis. One of the young men had taken the phone from her, informed the dispatcher of their presence on the scene and then disconnected the call. The other had snapped an oxygen mask over her father's face and began taking his vital signs. They were friendly and calm and did all they could to temper the situation.

The man who had taken the phone from her asked if she planned to accompany them to the hospital. Nerves nearly made her laugh at the idea that he thought she might remain at home while her father was being treated for a heart attack in the ER, but she guessed he may have seen stranger things while doing his job. When she didn't seem to catch on, he finally came right out and gently suggested she change into street clothes. Lauren had apologized and thanked him on the same breath, and then she'd run upstairs.

The soft blue paint on the waiting room walls was meant to instill tranquility, she was sure. But nothing short of news—and good news at that—would calm her anxiety. She strode to the window, crossing her arms over her chest, grasping her forearms tightly in some vain attempt to hold herself together.

"Are you Mr. Hunkavic's daughter?"

Lauren whirled around. "Yes. That's me. How is he?"

"About the same." The man in the green scrubs looked too young to be a doctor. "We think it's his heart, but it's too soon to tell. I've ordered tests. I just wanted to let you know we've notified the on-call heart specialist. And Mr. Hunkavic requested we call Dr. Amos. I tried to explain that he isn't on-call tonight and that he may not come, but your father insisted. Several times."

Good for you, Dad, she thought, happy to hear that he was feeling well enough to be a pain in the backside. She wished she hadn't been so upset that calling Doc hadn't even entered her head. She faced down muggers and thieves and wife beaters in court on a regular basis. She'd have thought she'd have more of her wits about her during an emergency.

But this was different. This was personal. This was her father.

"Thank you," she murmured, watching the young doctor until he disappeared behind the metal doors. Then she turned back to look out into the night. The yellowy light from the streetlamp threw a sickly glow over the street. Dead leaves tumbled and fluttered on the autumn breeze.

Her dad had always been such a strong, healthy man. What if this heart attack stole his strength? His health?

His life?

Her inhalation grew jerky and her eyes burned, but she willed herself not to cry. Come on, Lauren, she silently ordered. Don't you dare fall apart.

Her father needed her to be strong.

She perched on the edge of a blue plastic chair, gazing across the room but not seeing a thing. All she had to do was wait until the doctors work their magic. Then they'd bring her good news.

But what if the news wasn't good?

The question had her scrambling for her purse. If bad news came... the worst news... she didn't want to be alone. The cell activated with a well-practiced swipe of her thumb. There was only one person who loved her dad as much as she did. She found the contact by rote, not giving herself a chance to think about what she'd say or how he might respond.

After two short rings, he answered with a sleepy, "'Lo?"

"Greg—" his name raked from her throat painfully "—I know you're angry with me, and I have no right to ask. But I'm in the ER with Dad. Will you come?"

* * *

Simply knowing he was on his way had been enough to sustain Lauren through the fifteen minutes or so that it took him to arrive. She kept her eyes trained on the glass entryway, and when the automatic doors opened and Greg walked in, she decided she'd never seen a more welcome sight.

He was wearing the same clothes she'd seen him in at the barn earlier this afternoon, but that was okay because she'd tossed on the same pants and top she'd been wearing, too. His hair was wet, and she imagined he'd splashed water on his face to wake up. Whiskers shadowed his strong jaw.

She stood and waited for him to reach her.

"What happened?" Greg asked.

"Heart attack, they think." She bit her bottom lip to keep it from trembling. The fact that he was here, even after she'd treated him so badly today was enough to send her emotions into chaos. "Someone came out to say his condition is about the same. That they've called a heart specialist. And Doc." She smoothed an agitated hand over her cheek. "Dad must be scared, Greg. He asked them to call Doc."

Privy to the argument between the two men, Greg's dark brows rose, but he obviously tried to keep his alarm under control.

"Doc'll calm him down. Sit down. You look beat." He sat, and she settled in the chair beside him.

"The television woke me," she said. "I went downstairs and found him." The memory of her dad's appearance had her shaking her head. "He looked awful. White as a sheet, sweaty and he couldn't seem to breathe. Said he was in pain, and he was clutching at his chest." She closed her eyes. "God, Greg, I was scared to death."

"It's going to be okay." He reached out and placed his hand on her shoulder for a long moment then shifted to rest his arm on the back of her plastic chair. "He's right where he needs to be."

"I probably shouldn't have called you, but—"

"I'm glad you called, Lauren," he cut her off. "Lew is like a father to me. I want to be here."

She was too shaken to smile, but what he said eased some of the guilt she felt about waking him in the middle of the night.

"I feel so bad." She rubbed her palms together just to have something to do with her hands. "I should have been watching him closer. I can't remember the last time he went in for a check up. He had that silly argument with Doc, and he refused to call him or go see him. And you know how he's always complaining about some strange ailment or another."

Greg's mouth flattened and he nodded.

"I blame that computer of his," she said. "It's made him so preoccupied with every ache and pain. He surfs the internet just looking for illnesses to—"

"It's not the computer."

She shot him a look of disbelief. "Sure, it is. Have you seen his list of bookmarks? He must have a dozen different medical sites that he visits."

A smile curled the corners of Greg's mouth, and Lauren's gaze darted from his eyes to his lips.

"You don't remember that book he used to keep at his elbow?" Greg's grin widened. "The three-inch-thick tome that listed every illness and disease known to man?"

A hazy memory hovered and then clearly formed. "I'd forgotten."

Greg shifted so he could more easily look at her. "I could be wrong, but I always thought your dad's preoccupation with his health was a bid for attention."

"Of course, isn't that what every hypochondriac is hoping for? Attention from his friends and—"

"From you, Lauren. Specifically. Attention from you."

She straightened her spine. "I always paid him plenty of attention." Her voice went soft and her words formed slowly as she asked, "Didn't I?" The question was more for herself than for Greg.

During a good part of her adolescence, it had just been her and her dad. Why would her father think he needed to vie for her attention by conjuring medical maladies?

You're too independent, he'd told her.

Then she remembered something else he'd said. He'd complained about having to be creative to get her attention.

"I'm sure you have," Greg told her.

"Something's telling me you don't really believe that."

He lifted a shoulder and then let it drop. "You have been known to blow him off when he complains."

"But he's so silly most of the time, Greg. 'My hair hurts,' or 'my fingernails are splitting.' Like a hangnail is going to kill him." She immediately blanched at her choice of words.

"What you don't seem to understand," Greg said, "is that the ailment isn't the point. He just wants you to show a little concern. It's your time he's looking for."

She studied him for a moment, letting the words sink in. Then her gaze meandered over to the metal doors and she wondered what was going on behind them. "I hope I get a chance to give him some."

"Come on, now," Greg said. "Don't talk like that."

They sat silent for several minutes. CNN blared from the television across the room. Although worry continued to gnaw at her, she did feel calmer. She felt enormously grateful that she wasn't alone.

She got up and paced to the window, then back again. She paused, taking a moment to look at her ex-husband. Then she sat down again, this time on the coffee table, facing him, so close to him that their knees touched.

"Greg," she began, "I owe you a huge apology. I'm really sorry about the things I said out at the barn. I was an ass. And I hope you'll forgive me."

He looked at her for a moment, his dark eyes unreadable, then his gaze slid from hers and he looked at the floor.

If he chose not to forgive her, she couldn't blame him. She'd been rude and judgmental and arrogant.

"All the pieces were there," she admitted softly, reaching out and putting her hand on his knee. "And I didn't put it together. I was holding a large sum of money. Your money. Money that you had to have earned since the store folded, because I know that cost you everything. Yet I accused you of working for free. I don't know why I didn't see—"

"Lauren, do you think I wanted to lose my father's hardware store?" He reared his head and gazed steadily into her eyes. "He put his whole life into that business. Seeing the store go under would have disappointed him so much, I can't even find words to describe it."

Sadness seeped into his features, softening his jaw and the muscles around his mouth. He laced his fingers together, one thumb rubbing back and forth across the other.

"Do you think I didn't do everything in my power to save my business? My livelihood?" He shook his head. "The only thing that seemed to concern you was the fact that I didn't tell you what was happening. And what if I had, Lauren? What then? The big, smart lawyer could have saved the day when the idiot carpenter couldn't?"

"I never thought that." But even as the words tumbled from her mouth she knew her behavior over the past year or more totally belied them. She clearly saw on his face, in his eyes, that he realized it, too.

She looked away. Greg was the man she'd chosen to spend her life with, yet the moment he'd stumbled into trouble, she hadn't found it in her to be helpful. Or the least bit kind. No, the only things she'd found—and latched onto—had been blame and bitterness and anger.

The truth was hard to swallow. She hadn't divorced Greg because she'd stopped loving him. She'd divorced him because he'd failed.

What did that say about her?

The question was too big to wrap her mind around right here, right now. All she could think to do was drag her gaze to his and whisper, "I'm sorry. I truly am."

But it sounded feeble and insufficient.

Not knowing what else to say, Lauren went quiet and moved to the chair beside him. She slid as far back into it as the hard plastic would allow. She huddled there, nursing her misery and angst, her worry and fear, barely cognizant of the news anchor spouting off a story of death and destruction in some war-torn country, and then delivering a dire report about the world economy.

The double doors leading into the bowels of the ER swung open and every head, every eye, in the waiting room turned.

The sight of Doc Amos had Lauren on her feet in an instant.

"Doc?" Every ounce of trepidation she felt was expressed in her quaky voice, she knew it, could hear it, but couldn't do a thing to control it.

Greg, too, must have heard what she was feeling because he did the most extraordinary thing. He rose from his chair, stood beside her, and took her hand in both of his.

His grip was firm and steady, and the strength he exuded seemed to leach through her chilled skin, bolstering muscle and tendon. The urge to thank him for being there for her hovered at the periphery of her brain, but her need for information about her father kept her focus riveted to Doc.

The older gentleman sported a thick thatch of wavy white hair and a neatly trimmed snowy beard that, Lauren had always thought, would make him a perfect understudy for St. Nick. His blue eyes were bright and shining, and even though she knew he wouldn't be smiling if he had bad news to deliver, she still wanted to hear the actual words.

"He's okay, honey," Doc told her. "He's resting."

Her knees threatened to give way. She released a pent-up breath. Evidently sensing her rubbery-muscled relief, Greg slid his arm around her shoulder. She closed her eyes and leaned toward him, savoring the solid mass of him.

God, I love this man. The notion skittered through her brain and had almost vanished before she even realized she'd thought it.

"How bad was the heart attack?" Greg asked.

"Well, all the tests aren't back yet." Doc ushered them over to a cluster of nearby chairs and sat down, motioning for them to do the same.

Greg let go of her and slid one of the chairs closer to Doc for her.

"The ER guy did a great job," Doc said. "He ordered a full blood panel. But that won't be back for at least another hour. However, the EKG they performed was normal. Dr. Johnson, the heart specialist, is going over that now."

"Normal?" Lauren slid to the edge of the seat.

"That's good, right?" Of course, it was good, but she felt senseless at the moment.

Doc nodded. "Very. In fact, it's fairly conclusive that he didn't have a heart attack."

"Oh, Doc," Lauren breathed. "Those are wonderful words to hear."

"So what happened?" Greg was frowning. "Lauren said Lew was in bad shape when she called for an ambulance."

Again Doc nodded. "His pulse was through the roof when they brought him in. They'd gotten it down by the time I arrived." He chuckled. "And my appearance didn't do it any good, I'll say that. Lew didn't want me to examine him since he had started feeling better, but between me and the attending, we were able to talk him into it."

Lauren knew nobody did bullheaded as well as her father.

"I talked with him a while." Doc absently repositioned the stethoscope that was stuffed into the chest pocket of his lab coat. "At first, all he wanted to do was brag about his new girlfriend. Come to find out, I know her. She's a friend of Katie's."

Lauren nodded. "Norma Jean works for me."

"Seems that Lew and Norma went a little

overboard tonight," Doc said. "They had dinner and dessert. Death by Chocolate, Lew called it. And they talked over three cups of coffee. Each." Humor twinkled in Doc's eyes as he looked at Lauren. "I think your dad overdosed on caffeine."

"But he had chest pain," she told him.

"Indigestion from the chocolate." Doc planted his hands on his knees. "Antacids fixed that right up."

Lauren rolled her eyes.

Greg and Doc were smiling, and Lauren could only shake her head.

"I wanted to keep him overnight, just to be on the safe side." Doc got up from the chair. "But he won't hear of it. Says he wants out of here. Claims he's got a date at the Boys and Girls Club with Norma and he needs to get home to catch a couple hours sleep. I promptly told him no one likes a braggart."

Greg and Lauren both stood.

"I did tell him he'd have to stay until we get the blood results. Just as a precaution." Again, Doc unwittingly reached for the stethoscope, as if unconsciously battling a bad habit of losing track of it. "But you can come back and sit with him while he waits." As he talked, he turned and started for the metal doors.

Lauren made a move to follow him, but Greg put a hand on her arm.

"I think I'm going to take off," he said.

She looked at him, surprise forcing her to blink.

Before she could respond, Doc reached out his hand to Greg. "It was good seeing you again, Greg. Too bad it had to be in the wee hours of the morning."

The men chuckled as they shook hands.

"I'll see you inside," Doc said to Lauren, then he tucked his hands into the pockets of his lab jacket and traipsed away.

The idea that Greg would leave now confused Lauren. "You don't want to come in and see Dad?"

"Nah. Doc said he's okay." He avoided meeting her gaze. "You go ahead in. I'll touch base with Lew this weekend. I'll be sure to give him what for about all that caffeine."

He turned to leave, and she felt suddenly and strangely panicky. She reached out and touched his sleeve. The cotton fabric was warm from his body and his forward momentum tugged it from her grasp. But he did stop and look at her.

"Greg." She went quiet. Moistened her lips. Frowned. "Thank you. For everything."

His black eyes held hers for only an instant, and then he nodded before heading for the door leading out to the street.

As she watched the automatic doors open and Greg walk out of the hospital, her insides felt like a tightly coiled spring. She'd divorced the man, berated him, bad-mouthed him, been rude to him, verbally wounded him, yet after a single phone call, he'd come to her.

He was a good man.

But she had always known that. Somewhere inside, she had. Things had gotten in the way, is all. Her anger. Her inability to forgive. Her sheer and utter stupidity. Everything that had been blinding her had dissolved in the last hour or so. Here under the blaring lights of the ER waiting room, she was once again able to see Greg as the man she had fallen in love with, the man she had chosen to marry.

In the very instant that the night swallowed Greg in darkness, Lauren realized she was in deep trouble. She'd ruined everything, made a terrible blunder. And it was a mistake that couldn't be fixed. In leaving, in refusing to accompany her back into the exam room, he had sent her a clear and obvious message.

They were no longer a couple. No longer a family.

Chapter Seventeen

You're giving me the, 'It's not you, it's me' routine?
I *invented*, 'It's not you, it's me.'
Nobody tells me it's them, not me.
If it's anybody, it's *me*!
~George Costanza

Lauren shuffled the bags, cups, purse and briefcase she carried so she could open her office door. She'd run into a friend at Starbuck's and now her day was starting fifteen minutes off schedule.

"Morning, Norma Jean. Brought you a chocolate chip muffin and a latte." She huffed to catch her breath.

"Ooo, chocolate chip." Norma waggled 'give me, give me' fingers at Lauren. "My favorite."

"Sorry, I'm late. Is Margaret in my office?"

"Relax." Norma opened the little brown sack, indulging in a deep inhalation. "She canceled."

"But we're meeting with opposing counsel next week to discuss division of assets." Lauren had unloaded on Norma's desk and was untying the sash of her trench coat.

"Apparently, the Shanahans reconciled this weekend." Norma pulled a napkin out of the bag. "You're free until ten fifteen."

The coat slipped from her shoulders and she caught it. She stood there looking at Norma. "I guess, that's good news. For them, anyway." Then she went to the closet. "Might as well go ahead and work up Margaret's bill."

When she turned around Norma was popping the lid off her coffee. "How's Lew this morning?"

"Much better," Lauren told her.

His visit to the ER two nights ago had worn him out and he'd had to cancel his volunteering session at the Boys and Girls Club. Norma had stopped to check on him on her way home from the computer class, but he'd been napping.

"We ordered de-caf," Norma said for what must have been the tenth time.

They had both sworn as if under oath that they

believed their waitress had served them regular coffee by mistake after dinner. Norma had complained of insomnia, too.

"Stop," Lauren said softly. "I believe you."

Norma sipped her latte. "Mr. Minuteman called already this morning."

Lauren instantly knew to whom Norma was referring, and she was pleased with her self-control. Her lips barely twitched. Reacting to the nicknames Norma thought up for Scott would only encourage the incorrigible woman. Ever since Lauren had revealed his less than spectacular bedroom skills, Norma had conjured some extremely inventive monikers.

Fast Freddie. Pronto Pete. Mr. Rapid Rod. Hypersonic Howie. The Winged Weiner. Hair-trigger Harry. Although the list was obviously a work in progress, one name still stood out among the rest. Lauren had nearly spewed tea out her nose when she'd read Norma's memo, alerting her she'd had a telephone message from Mr. Two Shakes.

"I don't think he believed me when I told him you weren't in yet."

Lauren pried the lid off her chai tea and then snitched a pinch of Norma's muffin. "I really am going to have to break down and talk to him." She munched the moist cake, savored the rich chocolate as it melted on her tongue.

"He's determined to see you," Norma told her. "He scheduled an appointment."

Lauren couldn't believe her ears. "Here?"

Norma looked at her as if to ask, where else? "Said he was willing to pay a consultation fee if it meant he could talk to you."

Lauren shook her head. "I haven't put him off that long, have I?" Without waiting for an answer, she shot Norma a look. "Did you give him an appointment?"

Again, Norma nodded. Then she grinned. "A week from this Thursday."

She laughed. "Now that's low. I'll call him—"

The front door opened and who walked in but Mr. Two Shakes, himself. A double dose of adrenalin surged through Lauren. The first, caused by the fact that she'd been avoiding the man like a bad case of fleas, and hearing that he'd made an actual appointment in order to see her, she knew that he knew it. The second, due to his walking into the middle of a conversation where he was the hot topic.

"Morning, ladies."

She nodded and immediately lifted her cup to her mouth to cover her too-rigid smile.

Rejecting prospective clients was a skill at which she'd become adept. Telling some people no was a necessity if she wanted to keep her good standing in the legal community, so why she was balking at facing Scott was beyond her. Probably because the clients she turned away wanted her to break the law or act against good moral judgment, whereas she couldn't come up with a viable reason to stop seeing Scott. Well, she had a viable reason, but not one she felt comfortable communicating to him. Telling a man his 'technique' was lacking was something no woman wanted to do.

"How have you been, Lauren?" On the same breath, he added, "I've missed you."

The plastic smile that had taken her lips hostage refused to budge. "Hi, Scott. I've been well."

When a beat passed and she didn't say anything more, his blue eyes took on a whipped-puppy defenselessness.

"I was hoping you could give me five minutes."

Her heart thudded. "Wish I could, but—"

"Three minutes?" he countered.

Lauren didn't dare make eye contact with Norma.

"Oh, go on, Lauren," Norma chided gently. "Give the man three minutes. I'm sure he'll be quick."

Her gaze flew to Norma's face and she saw a wicked and teasing light dancing in the women's brown eyes and on her twitching lips.

"Scott, let's go back to my office," she said, amazed that she could get the words out without bursting out laughing. She ushered him down the short hallway. Hurting Scott wasn't something she wanted to do, and if she could avoid it, she would. She was just closing the door when he spun around to face her.

"I've got some great news," he told her. He reached into the inside breast pocket of his suit jacket and pulled out what looked like a business card. "I've found a woman who's interested in your carousel figures. She's a dealer. She's got one consignment shop in Frederick and two in the DC area. I showed her pictures and—"

"Pictures? How'd you get pictures?"

He looked momentarily chagrinned. "I went out there. To the barn. I tried to call you to ask if it was okay, but... well, we kept missing each other, and then, well—" he shrugged "—I just wasn't able to reach you."

"I've been really busy," she said.

His mouth flattened, but he said nothing.

Lauren's attention focused on his mouth and she wondered for what must have been the thousandth time how someone who melted her insides with a kiss could be so lousy between the sheets.

"Anyway, I, ah," he continued, softly, "showed this woman the horses and carnival animals she was very excited. Said she thought the restoration looked to be top rate and that you could get a good price for them."

When she made no move to take the business card from him, he set it on her desk. Lauren tucked a strand of hair behind her ear and then crossed her arms under her breasts. "Scott, I'm... surprised. I can't believe you've gone to all this trouble."

"You said from the start that you wanted to sell the figures." He lifted his hands, palm up. "I thought you might appreciate... my doing something to—" again he gestured with his open hands "—help."

Please don't dump me, is what she read in his tone. She sighed. "Scott, I do appreciate what you've done. I do, but... you see... the thing is... "

"You don't want to see me anymore." He blurted

the words as if he was pulling out a splinter so it wouldn't pain him any longer.

Again, she sighed. She was going to have to address this issue at some time. She was going to have to tell him that he was right; she didn't want to see him anymore. She only hoped he didn't want an explanation. But then she said, "I'm not selling the figures."

"Oh." He was taken aback.

A half smile stole over her lips, accompanied by a laughter that bubbled up from out of nowhere. Wow. She felt as surprised as he looked. The idea of not selling the animals hadn't entered her head, but now that the words were out, it felt too right not to be... right.

"So what are you going to do?" he asked.

She shook her head, her smile widening. "You know, I have no idea at the moment. But I'm not too worried about it. Something will come to me."

He nodded and then just stood there watching her; after a moment he slid his hands into his trouser pockets. "So... where exactly do we stand? You and I."

As far apart as possible, she thought.

"You want to have dinner tonight?"

She glanced toward the window, then back at

him. He deserved her undivided attention. She shook her head and kept her tone as gentle as possible as she murmured, "I'm sorry, Scott."

"Aw, Lauren." His exhalation was forced. "I knew it. What happened? I thought things were going great. We went out for some great meals. We laughed. We even had some sex."

Lauren dipped her chin and scrubbed at her forehead with her fingertips, banishing from her mind the image that he was offering her a Tic Tac.

"We had fun together, didn't we?" he pleaded.

She steeled herself and looked into his face. "Scott, you're a great guy."

"So... what?" Misery bit into his brow. "Tell me what I did to put you off."

She opened her mouth, but then closed it again without speaking. How on earth was she supposed to explain when the truth would only hurt him?

Putting on her best lawyer-like face, she said, "It's just that I've decided I'm not ready to date. It hasn't been all that long since my divorce was finalized. I thought I was ready, but... as it turns out, I'm not." He looked dubious. So much so that she felt the need to add, "Believe me, Scott. It's not you. It's me."

His broad shoulders fell. "Yeah. Okay. I guess."

For a moment, she feared he was going to press the issue, but then he raked his fingers through his tawny hair and offered her a goofy grin.

"It was good while it lasted, huh?"

She smiled. "It was." Allowing him a little dignity wouldn't hurt anyone.

He moved to leave and she took a side step to let him pass. He opened the door and then paused with is hand on the knob. "Maybe I'll see you around?"

"Maybe."

But they both knew that wouldn't happen. Scott slowly drew the door closed behind him, and Lauren heaved a sigh. But his plea instantly echoed in her head.

Tell me what I did to put you off.

Could he really not know? Could he be oblivious to what had happened between them in his bedroom?

Tell me what I did...

"Damn," she whispered aloud. "He doesn't know."

She covered her mouth with her fingertips, let them slide slowly down over her chin, off her face, her mind whirling. The voices of all the women Scott would date in the future seemed to cry out to her, begging her to set straight this man's sexual sonar. Before she could mull over any second thoughts that might dissuade her, she yanked open the door.

"Scott," she called, stopping him in his tracks.

He turned around to face her.

"I have three pieces of advice."

He went utterly still.

"Practice self-control. Slow way down." She paused, hoping against hope that he understood the message. "And pay attention to your partner."

He blanched, his forehead smoothing, his spine straightening.

Flames of mortification were just beginning to lick at his neck and face when Lauren closed her office door and leaned her back against it. She'd embarrassed him, yes. But she'd also been honest about his problems.

She could almost hear the women in his future applauding.

Chapter Eighteen

I got gaps. You got gaps.
We fill each other's gaps.
~Rocky Balboa

Lauren was still reclining against her office door when she heard the soft knock from the other side.

"He's gone," Norma Jean told her. "He sure didn't look happy. You okay, in there?"

Releasing her tightly folded arms, Lauren turned and let Norma in.

"Yeah." She exhaled a sigh. "But that wasn't easy. For either of us."

Norma shook her head. "Lord, his face was beet

red. He ignored me completely when I told him to have a great day."

Lauren walked to the center of the room, stretching the kinks out of her neck and shoulders. The encounter had her muscles as tight as a coiled spring. "It's over," she told Norma. "I broke it off, neat and clean."

As neat and clean as any break up could be, that was. Lauren combed her fingers through her hair, her blonde locks flying back as she stared out the window.

"What's wrong?" Norma tapped the pen in her hand against her fingers. "I know you're not upset about setting things straight with—"

"No. No," she rushed to say before Norma Jean had a chance to insult Scott with another nickname. "It's not that." To keep her hands busy, she flattened her palms together and smoothed them back and forth.

"Well, what is it? You look like you're going to crawl out of your skin."

Sighing, she said, "It's Greg."

"Lew told me he'd come to the hospital."

Lauren nodded. "He did. Even after I'd said some horrible things to him earlier that day. I was scared, Norma. Dad looked so sick. So I called

Greg, and he didn't hesitate. He came to the hospital even though he didn't have to; even though he wasn't obligated. I, um... he made me realize a few things."

A few things? What an understatement. He had shined a bright beam of light on who she was and how she'd been behaving. And it hadn't been pretty. Yet he'd come when she'd been afraid and alone.

"Anyone else would have told me to stuff it. But Greg... didn't."

Norma smiled. "Of course he came. He's family."

She shook her head. "That's just it. He was there just long enough to get me through. Then he left. He didn't even come back to the room to see Dad when Doc said we could. It was like Greg was sending me a message. He came when I called because that's the kind of person he is. He's a good man. But he didn't hang around like, well, like family would. He left as soon as he could. As if to point out that... we're not a couple anymore."

Norma softly remarked, "I'm confused. Why would that upset you? You're not a couple anymore, hon." Gently, she added, "That was your choice. In fact, you've felt pretty strongly about it."

Lauren worried her bottom lip between her

teeth. "It felt so final, Norma. Watching him walk away made me feel... " What she'd experienced that night had been so wretched that she couldn't describe it. "The timing is just bad because, well, I've realized I still have feelings for him."

Feelings, nothing. She still loved the man. Looking at Norma Jean, Lauren saw that she'd stunned her friend into silence.

"It's just as well, I guess." She walked across her office, rounded her desk and sat down. "We're too different to be together. If I was up, he'd be down. If I was left, he'd be right. Our life was crazy. Our marriage was pure chaos." She waved her hands in dismissal. "I've just got to get over myself. Greg's made his peace. I have to make mine."

"Now, hold on just a minute." Two steps brought Norma to the desk, front and center. "Different isn't necessarily bad. My Harry—may he rest in peace—was as different from me as night is from day. But we got along well. We had a great, crazy life together." Norma shoved the pen behind her ear. "Crazy can be good. Why, just look at me and your dad. Our personalities are poles apart, honey. You said it yourself. Yet we have a blast when we're together."

Norma bent at the waist and rested her hands

on the desktop. "Nature is made up of nothing but opposites, Lauren. Summer and winter, day and night, wet and dry, hot and cold. If the sun shined all the time, we'd never have a chance to appreciate the moonlight." She grinned. "And, sweetheart, heavenly things happen in the moonlight." Her chuckle was throaty, then she sobered. "Hold on. Lost my train of thought. What was my point?"

Lauren smiled despite the dejection she felt. "Opposites?"

"Oh, yes. Opposites allow differences to shine." She frowned. "That didn't make much sense, did it?" Then she tried again. "A woman's best characteristics never have a chance to stand out if she's with a person who has those same characteristics. And vice versa, of course." Norma straightened. "Am I making any sense?"

Back in the far reaches of Lauren's mind, a memory floated, hazy as a foggy day. A 'chick flick' date. A movie that had sparked a spirited discussion between her and Greg. Lauren zeroed in on the recollection, and the instant it came into sharp focus, the blood drained from her face.

"Oh, honey," Norma Jean said. "I've only confused you more."

Lauren looked up at Norma, her heart feeling

like it was melting in her chest. "Oh. Oh, Norma Jean," she breathed. "I realize what he was doing. I finally understand what he was trying to show me." She shoved her chair back, the wheels grating against the oak floor, and she tugged open the desk drawer with such force the contents rattled. "I can't believe I didn't see it. All this time. Wasted. I didn't understand."

"What? What didn't you understand?"

Scrambling around in the shallow drawer, Lauren latched onto the small key she'd been looking for and curled her fingers around it. She stood up so quickly she sent her desk chair thumping into the wall.

"Norma, I've got to run out. To the bank and..." Her gaze flitted across the furniture surfaces in search of her purse. The instant it dawned on her that she'd left everything on Norma's desk, she made a bee line for the reception area.

"Lauren, wait." Norma followed on her heels. "What about your ten fifteen?"

"I'll be back in time." She snagged her purse by the handle without stopping. "I hope."

But she couldn't worry about that right now.

"Lauren! Your coat!"

"I'll be fine," she called, but she was already out

on the sidewalk and feared Norma might not have heard. Oh, well. She could explain her haste when she returned.

She dashed across the street to the bank and, thankfully, didn't have to wait long for Marsha, the branch manager, to let her have access to her safe deposit box. She pulled two envelopes from the metal box, then grinning wickedly, she extracted a third.

Greg wasn't the only one who could make grand gestures.

After thanking Marsha, Lauren headed out of the bank, her smile slipping. What if she was too late? What if he'd had all he could take? What if she'd worn his patience clean out and he'd washed his hands of the whole mess they'd made of their lives?

The answer to all those questions, she guessed, was that she'd end up looking stupid. But she'd been acting stupid for a very long time, so another few minutes of it wouldn't hurt too much, now, could it?

She started her car and realized she had no idea where she was going. But a resourceful lawyer always knew where to find the answers she needed. Flipping open her cell, she phoned her father.

"Hey, dad," she said when he answered. "Where's Greg today?"

"Aw, Lauren, would you back off? What'd he do now?"

"Dad, he didn't do anything. I want to talk to him."

"You've got his number."

"I do, but I want to see him, Dad." Then she revised, "I want to surprise him."

"With what?" The gruff words toted a thick coat of suspicion.

Lauren gritted her teeth. "It's a surprise, Dad. If everyone in the world knows about it, that would kind of take away the ta-da factor, don't you think?"

"Now, Lauren, I'm not everyone in the world."

She shook her head. Her irascible father had obviously fully recovered from his scary medical emergency.

"Dad," she said, softly, patiently, "do you know where Greg is or don't you?"

"As far as I know he's still working on that woman's garage. I think he said he was painting today."

"Are you sitting in front of your computer?"

"Where else would I be?"

"How about going to white pages dot com and looking up the address for a Jo Leigh Stapleton? Can you do that for me?"

She cranked up her car's engine and turned on the heater. Maybe she should have taken the time to heed Norma's warning about a coat.

"Have you found it, Dad?"

"Hold on, hold on. Our connection is high-speed, not supersonic. Here. It's loading now."

He rattled off the address and she thanked him before snapping the phone shut. Turning onto Third St, she headed toward Maplewood.

Not fifteen minutes later, she was cruising slowly down Jo Leigh's street. By the time she'd spied Greg's truck, she'd already driven past the colonial with the detached garage and had to back up several feet. She parked at the curb, gathered up the envelopes from the passenger seat and then paused long enough to look at her reflection in the rear view mirror.

"Well," she whispered, "here goes nothing."

Nothing ventured, nothing gained.

Out on the limb is the only place to find the fruit.

Leap and the net will appear.

Do something every day that scares you.

Wise men and women down through the ages had spent their lives conjuring encouraging words meant to urge people to take risks. That's where success and happiness, and yes, even greatness was found, all of them promised. Well, Eleanor Roosevelt would be proud as a flippin' peacock today, Lauren thought, because she was scared to death. Tramping up the driveway, she swiped her sweaty palms on the thighs of her trousers.

The wide opening of the garage, where a metal door would normally be, sported a heavy-duty, plate glass door on one side and a large window on the other, like any other business might have. Lauren rapped on the glass.

"It's open," Greg called.

She went inside and saw him climbing down off a step ladder, a paint roller in his hand and smears of white ceiling paint here and there decorating his shirt.

"Lauren."

Surprise lifted his tone. Clearly, she was the last person he expected to see. Lauren's stomach twittered.

"What's wrong? Is Lew okay?"

"Dad's good. Irritatingly good." She smiled. "I

called him to find out where you were and he had me clenching my jaw in two seconds flat."

The sight of Greg's grin made her heart thud against her ribs.

"Sounds like he's back to normal," he said.

She nodded. She crossed the royal blue carpet, stepping carefully to avoid the plastic drop cloths that were strewn about.

"You look good, Greg." He had no clue just how good; she had to make a conscious effort not to let her eyes rove the length of him. "You doing okay?"

His brow pinched the tiniest bit as he nodded. If nothing else, her showing up here had thoroughly confounded him, that was certain.

She looked around her. "This place is amazing. You've done a great job. Jo Leigh must be very happy."

The pinch tightened and he nodded again, but the motion was slower, more doubtful, this time. He bent and set the paint roller in the pan.

That 'new carpet' smell permeated the space, mingling with the heavy scent of wet paint. Vaguely, Lauren was aware that a car passed by outside. She glanced out the big front window at the street, then back at Greg, noticing for the first time the smudge of white paint on his chin. A nervous smile automatically curled the corners of her mouth.

No one can move this forward but you, she told herself. So move! She took a step closer to him as if physically prodded by the thought.

"Here," she said, offering him one of the envelopes she'd brought, "I want you to have this."

"What is it?" His dark eyes never left hers as he accepted her offering.

"It's the deed to the land. Out on Skeeter Neck." She flipped her hair back behind her ear. "But you need to know that it's worth a lot of money." Then she stressed, "A *lot* of money. So don't go giving it away." Realizing her comment might sound to him like an inferred criticism, she rushed to add, "Not that you would. It's just… " The rest of the sentence petered out.

"What'd you do?" He glanced at the manila envelope in his hand. "Strike oil out there?"

Lauren's chuckle sounded too jovial. "No, nothing like that. It's not the land, but the merry-go-round."

"Really?"

She nodded. "But the treasure is in the figures. In order to cash in, you'll have to dismantle it." One look at his expression had her adding, "Yeah,

I know. I kind of figured that's how you'd feel. But I just wanted to make you aware." Now that she'd mentioned the carousel horses and circus animals, another thought popped into her head. "Oh, and I plan to keep paying your friend to refurbish them. I want to do that for you."

Greg was looking at her as if she'd suddenly sprouted a second pair of ears.

"And here's your check." She handed him another envelope. "I never cashed it. And here—" she forced the final, largest envelope into his hand "—that's the deed to my house." She quickly amended, "Our house. You really should have fought me for it, you know." Then she told him, "I want you to have it. I want you to have it all."

While she spoke, the deep frown on his brow began to smooth and the consternation fogging his dark gaze cleared.

Quietly, he said, "You remembered."

His eyes were impassive and the smile on his mouth had disappeared, and anxiety so overwhelmed her that she was forced to look away. She only nodded in answer.

Not long after they married, they had watched a movie—a dark comedy about a divorcing couple's one-upmanship antics. It had sparked a lively conversation between them about the fine art of divorce. Lauren had claimed that she would fight for every penny that the law allowed. Greg, on the other hand, had claimed that he would hand over all that he owned; that if the two of them were ever to find themselves in divorce court, he could only imagine himself as the guilty party, and he would want to do everything he could to win her back.

"As I recall," she murmured, dragging her gaze to his face, "I was very annoyed with you that night."

Finally, his lips quirked and she knew he remembered, too.

He glanced at the envelopes. "Our tactics were always miles apart."

She studied his face for a moment, wondering how on earth she'd lived without this man in her life for all these months. The streak of paint on his chin shouted out for her to reach up and wipe it away. But she didn't dare. "We are different, that's the truth. But that wasn't why I was angry back then. I was irritated that you'd come up with a more romantic solution than I ever could have. While I was conjuring a cold-hearted outcome, you were thinking like someone who was... in love. You always did. No matter what, you always acted like a man who loved his wife. Like a man who was married—who intended to stay married."

Her compliment evidently discomfited him because he broke eye contact with her.

"I wasn't exactly sure I'd correctly pegged your motives," she told him, "remembering how you argued with Judge Brooks when he awarded me the land."

His gaze swung back to hers. "I'd intended to fix up the merry-go-round. Then I was going to surprise you with it. But the judge threw a wrench in those plans pretty quick."

They both fell quiet.

Finally, she said, "I just wish you would have explained what you were doing." Sudden emotion made breathing difficult.

"I couldn't." He reached out and curled his fingers around one ladder rung. "You had to figure it out, or not, all on your own."

A knot rose in her throat and she swallowed around it. "You gave me plenty of time."

He lifted a shoulder. "That's something I had plenty of. I had faith in what we had, Lauren. In the trust we'd built. I hoped it would be strong enough to see us through."

Like night and day. They were that different. She

was the kind of person who didn't like to take a single step until she could see and feel solid ground beneath her feet; whereas, he was happy to step out on nothing but a cloud of faith, to live on trust and hope.

"Greg, I was blind and selfish and stupid. It wasn't you I was disappointed in, it was the failure. I didn't know how to handle it, and I ended up handling it all wrong. I didn't stand by you when you needed me most. My behavior's been unforgivable, I realize that now. I'm sorry, and my greatest wish is that someday you'll find it in your heart to accept my apology. It probably won't be today, or tomorrow, but someday... someday, I'm praying you can forgive me."

Had those words just come out of her mouth? Wishing and praying? Maybe there was hope for her yet.

Exhaling a long, soft breath, she felt as if a huge weight had been lifted off her chest. She looked into his dark, steady gaze and was still unable to tell what he might be thinking or feeling. She'd done the best job she could do. When she had forced him into this hurtful game called divorce, he'd immediately lobbed the ball into her court. It had taken her over a year to recognize the ball for what it was and smack it back in his direction. The next move was his to make, and there was no way for her to tell if he was still interested in playing the game.

"Well, that's all I came to say." She lifted her hands and then let her palms slap her thighs lightly. "I have a client due at the office soon. So I should go."

She turned to leave but stopped in her tracks when he said her name. Lauren twisted back around to face him, a jumble of tense and daunting emotions filling her.

"If I were to accept your apology... " He let his fingers slide off the ladder, his hand coming to rest at his side. "If I were to forgive you, right here, right now, what might that mean?"

His gaze was intense, expectant but at the same time suspicious. That was understandable. She'd tossed the man out of their home, she'd filed for divorce, she'd pressed him into signing the legal papers a whole year before the law required it. She'd called him all manner of names, hurt him with her derisive attitude, her anger, her bitterness. No wonder he was wary.

She couldn't believe he'd lobbed the ball back into her court so quickly. She was going to give him the point, the set, the whole match. He deserved it.

The boldness that crept over her was strong, almost erotic. She sauntered toward him until there were mere inches between their bodies, and then she slid her hand up the length of his broad chest. The heat of him seeped through his shirt and sent her heart racing.

"If you forgive me," she whispered, leaning even closer, "I promise to spend the rest of my life trying to make you happy. I'll be the best wife I know how to be. And I will never—" she reached up and placed a soft kiss on his mouth "—ever—" she kissed him again "—lose faith in you again." Her lips twisted into a goofy, apologetic grin. "I can't stop being me, of course. So I can't promise I won't ever get angry, but I'll try really hard to—"

He cut off the rest of her sentence with a gentle press of his index finger against her lips. "Spending the rest of your life making me happy will be enough." He touched his nose to her temple, inhaling the scent of her, and when he next looked into her face, hunger sparked his onyx eyes. "I'd never want you to stop being you."

She melted into him. "You know... I didn't come here with this intention. I only came to make amends. I never expected... never imagined you might forgive me." She searched his eyes and breathed, "So quickly." His mouth closed over hers. His kiss was hot and moist and delectably possessive. A heady pulse thudded deep inside her.

When they parted, Lauren felt as if she'd run a marathon.

"I wish we could go home," she said, her voice husky and raw. "But I really do have clients coming to the office."

"And I promised Jo Leigh I'd finish this paint job today."

Chuckling, she rested her forehead on his chest, straining for time to collect herself. Then she looked up at him, sobering, searching his face, his gaze.

"I love you, Greg."

He hugged her to him, and the envelopes filled with a deed and money—a lifetime of mere 'stuff'—were cool against her back in contrast to heat of his hands and arms wrapped around her, enfolding her in security and love.

"I've been waiting a hell of a long time to hear you say that," he murmured just above her ear.

She leaned back, smoothing her hand over his shoulder, and he released her. In that moment, she felt oddly shy. Almost awkward. It was silly, really. This was Greg. The man who had forgiven her for so much. The one who'd had faith in their relationship all along. She'd known him almost half her life. Still, she couldn't shake the feeling that this was new. Different. Exciting.

Stepping away from him, she looked at the floor, and then into his face. She reached out and glided the pad of her thumb over the small comma of paint on his chin. "So... can I expect you home for dinner?"

"Regular time?" he asked, capturing her hand, opening her fingers and planting a kiss on the fleshiest part of her palm.

Blood throbbed through her body and she smiled. "Yeah. Regular time would be great."

Lauren didn't remember opening the door to leave. She didn't even remember walking out to her car; she supposed she floated the whole way. Pure, unadulterated happiness had a way of doing that to a woman.

Epilogue

I love being married.
It's so great to find that one special person
you want to annoy for the rest of your life.
~Rita Rudner

"Damn, now why'd you go and change the suit?" her dad groused.

Lauren chuckled at her father even though she was feeling a little glum. "Because I'm in this to win."

Wednesday evenings had become Father/Daughter Night. They'd have dinner together, and then either she or her dad would pick an activity that allowed them to spend some quality time together. Tonight, her father had chosen to meet at her house and play Crazy Eights, even though he and she both knew it had been her turn to choose. He'd also invited Norma Jean, as well as Doc and Katie Amos.

Lauren wasn't feeling sullen because it was Wednesday; she'd actually come to look forward to the hump-day evenings spent with her dad. And her 'mood' hadn't been caused by her father brazenly usurping her turn of selecting the night's entertainment. It wasn't even because she had to play hostess to a houseful of unexpected company.

Surliness hadn't struck until she'd arrived home from work and discovered, via her dad, that Greg had called to say he wouldn't be able to join them. Lauren had tried calling him twice, but both times his cell had gone directly to voice mail.

"I'm out!" Norma Jean whooped and shimmied her shoulders. "Count 'em up people!"

"Norma Jean, how could you do this to me?" Katie heaved a bosomy sigh and gathered the huge hand of cards the round had left her holding, her pudgy fingers nimbly tallying the points.

"Now, now, dear," Doc comforted her. "You win some, you lose some."

Katie looked from the stack of cards she

clutched to the three her husband held and offered up a good-natured, "Stuff it, Charlie."

"Put me down for twenty points," Lauren said, tossing her cards onto the pile. She slid her chair away from the dining room table and stood. "I'm going to the kitchen for more pretzels. Anyone want anything while I'm up?"

No one took her up on her offer and she schlepped off, amazed that she felt lonely with all these people around. It was ridiculous to miss Greg this much when she'd just seen him twenty four hours ago.

So much had changed over the three weeks (twenty five days, to be exact, but who was counting?) since they had reconciled. Her father was once again settled in his own apartment, although Lauren was fairly certain he spent most of his nights at Norma Jean's house. (She couldn't believe her dad was still having more sex than she was. Life, really and truly, wasn't fair.) He and Norma had become pretty much an item. So much so that Thanksgiving Day had been a warm but chaotic afternoon spent meeting Norma Jean's three grown sons, their wives and a whole slew of wild, running, yelling, laughing children. She and Greg had spent the day making eye contact and sharing silent and pointed messages; when Joey and Jimmy argued and had nearly came to blows over who would sit next to their grandmother during the meal, when Zoe had bumped into the edge of the dining room table and let out what seemed like a never ending wail, when Thomas and Melinda spilled their milk across the table, when that crystal candy dish went crashing to the floor and no one professed to know how it had happened. It had been one of the most fun holidays Lauren had ever experienced.

These weeks had also seen major developments in her and Greg's relationship. She'd suggested he immediately move back home, but he'd flat out refused. He'd thought they needed some counseling before they went back to cohabitating. Lauren had been impressed with his idea, but when the counselor had established a firm 'no sex' rule right off the bat, she'd almost shouted, "No way! No how!" To Greg, of course, not the counselor. However, she'd complied because she really did want learn how not to make the same mistakes they had the first time around. But just because she'd been abiding by the rules didn't mean she had to suffer in silence. This morning after their counseling session—the theme of which had been commitment—she'd joked to Greg that all her pent up horniness had her feeling like Hoover Dam. In response, he'd kissed her until she thought her bones were going to dissolve; which had only made her all the more lovesick and lusty.

So the recap was: her father, as crotchety as ever, was having sex, and she was not. And she and Greg were back together, almost. And her Big O problem was still... well, a problem. This was not the kind of happy ending she'd have expected. But then, she guessed, she was holding fast to that proverb coined by the guy who said the opera ain't over 'til the fat lady sings.

As if on cue, Katie Amos let out long, high-pitched note that was loud enough to curl the ends of Lauren's hair. She nearly dropped the bag of pretzel twists she was carrying in from the kitchen.

"After hearing that," Katie proclaimed with a sniff, "the church choir director had no choice but to give me a solo in the Christmas Cantata."

Lauren's cell chirped and she reached to unclip it from the waistband of her jeans. Greg's name glowed on the small display and she smiled.

"I've been worried about you," she greeted.

"Sorry. I've been working on a project most of the afternoon."

The mere sound of his voice made her pulse skitter. "Where are you?"

He sidestepped her question with one of his own. "Can you meet me?"

"Oh." She drew out the word until it sounded like whine. "I wish I could. But it's Wednesday. I've got Dad here. And Norma Jean. And the Amoses." Then she said, "You were supposed to be here, too."

"Sorry," he murmured into her ear.

And her heart pounded.

"Listen, ask Lew if he'd mind if you stepped out for awhile."

"Are you playing this hand or not, Lauren?" Her father called to her as he shuffled the deck of cards.

"Give me a sec, Dad." She hated to disappoint her father; their Wednesdays together had brought them closer than they'd ever been. Greg knew how important these evenings had become.

"I'd like for you to come," he urged, softly, "I've got something to show you."

Her breath caught and a shiver coursed from the top of her spine all the way to her tailbone. She hadn't heard those words in—good mercy, Ms. Percy—she couldn't say how long.

"Dad—" Lauren tried to tamp down the

excitement jolting through her "—would it be all right if I went to meet Greg for a bit? I won't be long." Immediately she asked Greg, "Will I be long?"

"Not too long," he hedged.

Her dad didn't even look up from the deal. "Sure. Go. I've got plenty of company."

Norma Jean and Doc and Katie scooped up their cards and began studying and rearranging the hands they'd been dealt.

"I don't think I'll be missed," Lauren told Greg, already heading for the coat closet by the front door. It probably should have dawned on her that Lew Hunkavic never missed a prime opportunity to gripe, but all she could think about was the surprise Greg had in store for her. "Where are you?"

"At the barn. Hurry."

Jeff Gordon would have been proud when she pulled onto the property a scant eleven minutes after leaving her driveway. A personal record, for sure.

Wavering light peeked through the gaps in the old barn's weathered exterior. A light dusting of December snow coated the ground. Lauren tugged open the wide-plank door just enough so that she could slip inside.

Her breath left her in a long, awestruck, "Ooohh." Dozens of candles flickered and danced, the squares of shiny metal sheeting he'd used as bases reflecting the light onto the walls and casting shadows in the rafters. The barn's interior glowed with a rosy mantle of soft, romantic radiance.

Greg stood by the merry-go-round, and their gazes caught and held as she made her way to him.

"Hey," she murmured finally, smoothing her hands over his chest and settling her palms on his broad shoulders.

"Hey, yourself."

He rested his hands on her waist, his thumbs slipping into the waistband of her jeans. It was a habitual action he'd preformed a thousand times during their married years, and she wanted to kick herself for becoming so lackadaisical back then that she'd take it for granted—taken him for granted. With a slight feline arch, she pressed the flat of her tummy to his. She wanted him to know she was on fire for him. His eyelids drooped slightly and desire sparked in his black as night eyes. The fact that she could elicit such a response from him was a powerfully seductive aphrodisiac.

Lifting on tip-toes, she placed a chaste kiss on his mouth. "I want you so badly, I can't stand it."

The need blazing in his eyes mirrored her own.

He kissed the tip of her nose and then asked, "Want to take a ride?"

Anticipation fluttered through her and she grinned wickedly.

"On the merry-go-round, silly." He set her several inches away from him. "Howie finished another horse. And it's a beauty. I rewired the outside switch, and greased the conveyer. I've replaced all the light bulbs and cleaned the music box."

The secretiveness lacing his smile had her curious.

"And I fixed the loading mechanism in the ring box and hung it over there on the post." He pointed. "What to give it a try?"

"I'd love to!" She didn't bother curbing her delight. This was just the kind of fun she'd expected from him.

Before mounting the newly refurbished Pinto, Lauren took a moment to admire the refinishing job. The pony had been given a mottled brown and cream coat, and the saddle and bridle touted brilliant silver studs.

It would be months before all the animals were finished and remounted, but the merry-go-round was really coming along. Greg had talked about opening the barn for a Saturday every month during the spring and summer to offer the kids from the Boys and Girls Club a full day of free rides. He dreamed of finding some old fashioned arcade games and maybe building a miniature golf course on the land surrounding the barn. Affordable entertainment was difficult to find in Sterling and Greg had a vision that would provide it.

Settling her foot on the flat metal pedal, she swung her left leg over the pony and picked up the bridle. "Ready," she proclaimed, the anticipation of capturing a brass ring putting a smile on her face.

"Hold on," he warned. "Here you go." He touched a button and the conveyer began to move.

The carousel picked up speed quickly with none of the thumping and bumping she'd experienced before. The horse undulated beneath her and the box holding the brass rings finally came into view. Lauren slid forward in the saddle. But at the last instant, she jerked her hand away, letting out a squeal when she saw what she took for a spider hanging from a silken thread at the bottom of the box.

She twisted for another look—spiders weren't shiny—but the post was already too far away.

A question flashed in Greg's dark eyes, his brows arched, when she came around and she had to shrug and confess, "I missed it."

On the second revolution, instead of focusing on the box that held the brass rings, she looked for whatever it was dangling from the string. She saw a glimmer of white, a gleam of gold. Grinning broadly, she reached out, and snatched it at the last second.

It was her ring. The diamond engagement ring Greg had given her when he'd first proposed. Happy tears burned her eyes, and when the merry-go-round brought her full-circle, she was surprised when the spot where Greg had been standing was empty. She shifted and turned, searching for him, and then she saw him weaving his way through the circus animals.

By the time she'd hopped off the Pinto, he was beside her and she wrapped her arms around him, the ring pressed tightly in her palm. She couldn't stop kissing him. Then he pulled back in sudden alarm, evidently having tasted the salty tears running down her face.

"You're crying."

"I'm happy," she told him. "And I'm scared thinking about what could have happened. What if I hadn't remembered that movie? Or the discussion we'd had? That was forever ago. What if I had stayed angry? What if you had gotten tired of waiting?"

He silenced her with a kiss. "No more 'what ifs,' okay?" Tugging her arms from around his neck, he fished the ring from her hand.

"How did you do this?" she whispered. The ring had been tucked away in a box that she'd put out of sight in a dresser drawer.

Greg chuckled. "Lew had one hell of time finding it for me."

"Dad?"

He nodded, smiling. "In on the whole thing. He'd found your rings a few days ago, and I was planning this shindig for Christmas. Then you said what you did today, and I decided tonight would be better timing." His tone went silky as he added, "I mean, you did say your dam was about to break."

She laughed. "I did, didn't I?"

His gaze caught and held hers. "So what do you say? Will you marry me? Again?"

Emotion swirled in her chest and words failed her. She nodded, holding out her left hand, and Greg slid the ring on her finger.

"You think Judge Brooks would marry us?"

She loved the idea. "I'm sure he will." Then a flash of guilt jolted through her, and the urge to tell him about her indiscretion with Scott made her frown. "There's something you should know."

He stroked her cheek, smoothed away her frown with his fingertips. "No," he whispered. "All I need to know is that you're here. With me." He kissed her eyebrow. "I'm not trying to hide my head in the sand. It's just that I've decided that whatever happened needed to happen." He kissed her cheek. "So you would know this is where you want to be."

Lifting her hands to his face, she brought his mouth to hers. Their kisses were steamy, their tongues teasing and tasting as if for the very first time.

She unfastened his belt and the button of his jeans, and then tugged his shirt from his waistband, her fingers hungry for the feel of him; the hardness of his muscles, the heat of his skin.

She shrugged out of her coat, their lips never breaking contact.

"It's not too chilly in here?" Worry nipped at his brow.

"It's hot." Her voice was raw with need. "Too hot."

She wanted this—wanted him—desperately, but when he unfastened several buttons of her blouse, she experienced a single moment of clarity. The last thing she wanted was for him to regret their actions, regret this night. She stilled his hands.

"What about Dr. Warren?" she asked. "What about the rules?"

Greg's reply required that their counselor take his rules and contort himself into a position that wasn't humanly possible. He made short work of the buttons on her blouse and slid the fabric off her shoulders. He nibbled a trail of hot kisses from the curve of her neck to the back of her ear.

"Greg," she whispered, "let's have a baby."

His head whipped up.

"Let's have a whole slew of babies."

He laughed. "You've lost your mind. After Thanksgiving, I thought—"

"I loved the madness," she told him.

He just looked at her in disbelief.

She silently mouthed, loved it. Then she murmured, "Almost as much as I love you."

He kissed her, long and slow. "Let's just take this one step at a time."

And then right there on the revolving carousel, with the freshly painted Pinto undulating at her back and candlelight burnishing their bodies, Greg solved her Big O problem. In fact, he solved it several times over.

Later—much, much later—when every muscle in her body had turned to rubber, every pent up stress dissolved away, every need sated, Lauren found herself smiling. They'd gathered up shirts and belts, underwear and shoes, and wearily dressed, both of them wearing silly smiles. She sat on the crossbar of the saw horse now, grinning down at her bare foot and then lifting her gaze to watch Greg scratch his head, cursing under his breath as he searched the carousel in vain for her missing sock.

Life and love, she decided, wiggling her chilly toes, were exactly like that merry-go-round. Blemished. Flawed. Imperfect. But with the right person by your side, it could be one hell of a ride.

# # #

A Note From The Author

Thank you for taking the time to read my book. I hope you enjoyed it. If you did, please consider telling your friends about The Merry-Go-Round or posting a review of it. Word of mouth from readers is an author's best tool for getting the word out.

If you would like information on new releases and sales, please sign up for my newsletter: http://madmimi.com/signups/110899/join

For more information about me and the books I've written, visit my website at:

www.DonnaFasano.com

I love to hear from readers!

All my best,

~Donna~

Other Books By Donna Fasano

Ocean City Boardwalk Series:
Following His Heart, Book 1
Two Hearts In Winter, Book 2
Wild Hearts of Summer, Book 3
An Almost Perfect Christmas, Book 4
Grown-Up Christmas List, Book 5
The Wedding Planner's Son, Book 6

~ ~ ~

Reclaim My Heart
The Merry-Go-Round
Her Fake Romance
Take Me, I'm Yours
His Wife for a While
Mountain Laurel

~ ~ ~

The Single Daddy Club Series:
Derrick, Book 1

Other Books By Donna Fasano

Jason, Book 2
Reece, Book 3

~ ~ ~

A Family Forever Series:
A Beautiful Stranger, Book 1
Made in Paradise, Book 2
A Reason to Believe, Book 3
An Accidental Family, Book 4
Nanny and the Professor, Book 5

~ ~ ~

Non-fiction Books
Cooking In All Directions
Prayer of Quiet
Favorite Christmas Cookies
Recipes of Love
Guy Food

About The Author

Donna Fasano is a USA TODAY Bestselling Author whose books have sold 4 million copies worldwide and have been translated into two dozen languages. She lives on Maryland's Eastern Shore with her husband.